The elevator came to a halt, and the doors slid open. A glance at the numbers confirmed that Marin still had four floors to go.

She stepped to the corner as a tall man entered and reached toward the buttons. Then he smiled in her direction. "Oh, both heading for the lobby. Good." He leaned into the opposite corner, the warm smile still lighting his face. "You look familiar. Have we met?"

Sounded like a pickup line. Only she wasn't in the mood to entertain, no matter how handsome this stranger. She didn't smile in return. "I don't believe so."

The man shook his head slowly, his brown eyes narrowing below thick, arched brows. He stood a good ten inches taller than Marin, and she stifled the urge to shrink into the woodwork. "No, really. You look very familiar. I know I've seen you—" Then his eyebrows shot high in recognition. "Is your father Darin Brooks?"

Now it was Marin's turn to raise her brows. "Y—yes. How did you know?"

He chuckled—a low, throaty sound that seemed comforting for some odd reason. "I knew I'd seen you. The pictures on his desk—a regular portrait gallery. You're Marin, right?"

Marin nodded. She gave the man a quick perusal. He didn't seem the executive type usually seen wandering through Branson Building. Worn Levis, a plaid shirt open at the collar—no tie—and brown hiking boots made up his attire. His brown hair was rather shaggy, longer at the collar and curling up around his shapely ears. He gave the rugged appearance of a lumberjack. What could he have been doing in Dad's office?

KIM VOGEL SAWYER, a Kansas resident, is a wife, mother, grandmother, teacher, writer, speaker, and lover of cats and chocolate. From the time she was a very little girl, she knew she wanted to be a writer, and seeing her words in print is the culmination of a lifelong dream. Kim relishes her time with family and friends, and stays active in her church by teaching adult Sunday school, singing in the choir, and being a "ding-a-ling" (playing in the bell choir). In her spare time, she enjoys drama, quilting, and calligraphy. She welcomes visitors to her Web site at www.KimVogelSawyer.com

Dear John

Kim Vogel Sawyer

Heartsong Presents

For Kaitlyn, whose loving heart is open to everyone.
   And with gratefulness to John, for showing me how to truly worship.

A note from the Author:
I love to hear from my readers! You may correspond with me by writing:

Kim Vogel Sawyer
Author Relations
PO Box 721
Uhrichsville, OH 44683

ISBN 1-59789-033-2

DEAR JOHN

one

Marin Brooks blinked twice and stared at her aunt. "Excuse me. What did you say?"

"I said"—Lenore's stiff lips barely moved—"I hope you will finally do the sensible thing and have John put in some sort of home."

Marin shook her head. Why would she bring this up now of all times? Marin's parents were dead only four days, the funeral was barely over, and already Aunt Lenore was hollering to "put John away."

This conversation had been played before, but it had always been Marin's mother on the receiving end of Lenore's opinionated comments. Her heart ached as the loss of her parents hit her again. In fact, she felt as if a boulder sat on her chest. Why couldn't Lenore give her time to heal before beginning that tiresome tirade about John?

"Aunt Lenore, you know how Mother felt about—"

"My sister spent every day of that boy's life taking care of him." Her aunt cut her off abruptly. "She worked herself into an early grave trying to make him more than he had the ability to be. Now she's gone—God rest her soul—and that responsibility falls to you." Lenore clutched Marin's arm, leaning in and whispering harshly. "Do the sensible thing, Marin. Put him in a home and get on with your life. Don't waste your life as my dear sister did."

Marin stared in amazement as Lenore released her arm and strode away, her chin held high, a fake smile plastered on her wrinkled face. The voices of visiting relatives and bereaved friends seemed to fade into the distance as Marin turned to focus her attention on John. He appeared so forlorn sitting in the middle of the sofa, his palms on his thighs, his face drooping as he watched the milling people who talked around him as if he weren't there. The boulder pressed harder. John was her responsibility now.

How she loved him.

And pitied him.

Sometimes the two emotions were so intermingled it was hard to choose one over the other. Her earliest memories involved John. How could she do what Aunt Lenore suggested? And how could she not?

Marin shook her head again, trying to clear it. She would have time to think of that later. Time when the funeral was officially over and people had gone home and she and John were alone. Then they could talk. Then she could think. There was too much noise, too much consoling, too much. . .sorrow. . .to add more to it now. There would be time. Because from now until her dying day, John would be her responsibility.

❧

"Marin, where are Mom and Dad?"

Marin looked up from her morning newspaper and offered a sad smile. "Remember, John? We talked about this. Mom and Dad are in heaven. They had an accident, and they went to heaven with Jesus. Remember?"

John nodded, his thin blond hair falling over his high forehead. His hazel eyes, flecked with gold and green, caught Marin's attention as they always did. John's every thought could be read in his almond-shaped eyes. She read fear and uncertainty now, and pity rose in her chest.

"You don't have to worry. Mom and Dad are happy and well with Jesus."

John's lower lip quivered. He poked at the toast on his plate with a stubby finger. "I miss them, Marin." His clipped, concise way of speaking seemed more pronounced in his sorrow. As always, his pronunciation of *r* came out like a *w*, making him sound much younger than his thirty-one years.

Marin felt maternal as she reached across the table and took his hand.

"I know. I miss them, too."

"I will not see them again."

Marin tugged his hand. "Yes, you will. We'll both see them again, when we get to heaven."

John's eyes lit up, the smile changing his countenance. "Can we go today, Marin? Can we go to heaven today?"

Marin felt tears prick her eyes. How she missed her mother! She had always known the best way to explain things to John. She could make him understand without hurting him. Marin was completely out of her league.

"No, I'm sorry, but we can't. You see—"

John threw her hand away, anger pursing his face. "You are mean, Marin. You are mean not to let me see Mom and Dad. I do not like you when you are mean." He rose and stood glowering at her.

Marin rose, too, reaching her hand to him. "John, it isn't that I don't want you to see Mom and Dad. I want to see them, too. But—"

John covered his ears and squinched his eyes. "No! I will not hear you, Marin. I will not listen!"

Marin sighed, and the tears that had threatened earlier now slipped free and rolled down her cheeks. *I can't do this, God! I can't take care of John. I don't know how. . . .*

Her father's voice slipped into her memory. "Marin, when your mother and I are gone, you will be all John has. We're counting on you to care for him." How many times had she heard those words? Countless times. But had she ever believed it would happen? Never. Their parents had been so healthy, so vital. Marin had heard the statement, agreed to it, but never once had she believed she would be twenty-three years old and left to care for her brother. Resentment built, but responsibility squelched it. She wouldn't let her parents down. She wouldn't let John down.

"Marin?"

John's voice intruded into her thoughts. She lifted her face to find that he had dropped his hands. His eyes now glittered with tears.

"Marin, being in heaven means dead." John's chin quivered as he waited for her to respond.

Marin wished so much she could deny the truth of his statement. She fought the sobs that pressed against her chest as she slowly nodded, tears raining down her cheeks.

John's anger dissolved, and he reached for her. "Do not cry, Marin. I am sorry."

"Oh, John—" Marin rounded the table and enfolded her brother in a hug. He clung, in need of comfort.

The problem was, Marin needed comfort, too. But the hug was all one-sided. John took comfort, and Marin gave it. And that was how it would be.

≈

Marin signed the last of the papers on the lawyer's desk then leaned back with a sigh. "I assume you will handle the funeral expenses and all of my parents' final bills then send me a check for the balance of Dad's insurance?"

Mr. Whitehead nodded, his snow-white hair shining in the sunlight that poured through the large plateglass window behind him. Had the situation been less somber, Marin might have giggled. Whitehead fit the man so well.

"That's correct, Miss Brooks. Your father was quite an astute businessman, and he left you very well provided for. Financial worries should be few." He linked his fingers and rested the heels of his hands on the edge of the highly polished cherry desk. "Would you like for me to arrange for the sale of Brooks Advertising?"

Marin set her chin. "No. I intend to run the advertising firm myself. I have my business and graphic arts degrees." A stab of pain struck as Marin remembered why her parents had been on the road the night of the accident. She shoved the memory aside—she didn't have time for that now. "I am qualified to step into Dad's shoes, and I intend to keep the business running. Of course"—she offered a shrug and a smile—"I'm counting on his employees to stick with me. If they bail, I might have a problem."

Mr. Whitehead returned her smile with one of his own. "In my estimation your father's employees were loyal to him and would transfer that loyalty to you. They are not eager to search for another place of employment." Then his expression turned serious. "But I do have a small concern. You are quite young, Miss Brooks, and the two top men in your father's employ have much more experience. You might consider, for your sake, making them partners in the business and leaning on their expertise. It would lighten your load considerably, which would be to your advantage, considering. . ." His cheeks mottled with pink as his voice drifted off.

Marin understood. "Considering I have John to care for as well?"

The man nodded, looking away. His cheeks blazed red now. Bringing back his gaze to meet Marin's, he continued in a gruff voice. "Miss Brooks, if I may be honest. . . ?"

Marin held her hand outward, inviting him to share his thoughts.

"You are a young, attractive, intelligent woman. Your father often shared his pride in you. He also shared his concern about his son. I believe your father would understand if you chose to find a suitable placement for John. Between the insurance settlement and the business, you will have adequate financial support for both yourself and your brother. If you would like for me to make inquiries about facilities that cater to the disabled, I would be more than willing to assist you."

Marin shook her head. "Mr. Whitehead, I appreciate what you're saying. Believe me, you aren't the only one who has expressed this thought." Marin's ears still rang with Aunt Lenore's daily harangue. "But I promised my parents

I would care for John, and I intend to do so at home, just as Mother did. There really is no other option. John would never understand why I was removing him from his home. He's lost Mom and Dad." Her throat tightened. "I won't take away his home, too."

Mr. Whitehead sighed. "I understand your position. But if you should change your mind. . ."

"I won't." Marin stood on that firm announcement and held out her hand. "Please let me know if I need to sign any other papers. I've left John too long. I need to be going now."

The lawyer rose and shook Marin's hand firmly. "I will be in touch. Good luck to you, Miss Brooks. And again, my condolences on your loss."

Marin nodded and left the office. She moved through the echoing hallway to the elevator and, alone behind the sliding doors, allowed herself a couple of minutes of sorrow. Condolences on her loss, Mr. Whitehead had said. Did anyone really understand everything she had lost? Her parents, her best friends, her encouragers, her Christian examples. . .and her short-lived independence.

How Marin had enjoyed college! The freedom to stay out late, to giggle with friends, to flirt with the handsome boys on campus. . . Only the family picture on her desk had intimated that Marin was different from the other girls. She had finally found the freedom to be young and carefree during the years at college, away from home and away from the responsibility of being the protector and teacher of her older brother.

"Carefree and young" had now abruptly ended before she was ready for it. *Why, oh, why did Dad have to pull out in front of that semi?* she wondered again. *Mom and Dad weren't old enough to die. . . .*

The elevator came to a halt, and the doors slid open. A glance at the numbers confirmed that Marin still had four floors to go. She stepped to the corner as a tall man entered and reached toward the buttons. Then he smiled in her direction. "Oh, both heading for the lobby. Good." He leaned into the opposite corner, the warm smile still lighting his face. "You look familiar. Have we met?"

Sounded like a pickup line. Only she wasn't in the mood to entertain, no matter how handsome this stranger. She didn't smile in return. "I don't believe so."

The man shook his head slowly, his brown eyes narrowing below thick, arched brows. He stood a good ten inches taller than Marin, and she stifled the urge to shrink into the woodwork. "No, really. You look very familiar. I know I've seen you—" Then his eyebrows shot high in recognition. "Is your father Darin Brooks?"

Now it was Marin's turn to raise her brows. "Y–yes. How did you know?"

He chuckled—a low, throaty sound that seemed comforting for some odd reason. "I knew I'd seen you. The pictures on his desk—a regular portrait gallery. You're Marin, right?"

Marin nodded. She gave the man a quick perusal. He didn't seem the executive type usually seen wandering through Branson Building. Worn Levis, a plaid shirt open at the collar—no tie—and brown hiking boots made up his attire. His brown hair was rather shaggy, longer at the collar and curling up around his shapely ears. He gave the rugged appearance of a lumberjack. What could he have been doing in Dad's office?

"I'm Philip Wilder. Your father helped me with some brochures for my business." The elevator doors slid open to the lobby, and Philip gestured for Marin to precede him. He followed her out and flashed another white smile. "He did great work. Tell him thanks again for me, will you?"

Before Marin had a chance to explain that his request would be impossible, he turned and trotted toward the double doors leading outside and disappeared. She felt somehow deflated by his departure. It was the first normal conversation she'd had since her parents' deaths. The first exchange that hadn't included condolences or John. It had felt good.

Sighing, she walked slowly to the exit. Maybe her only normal conversations would now come from strangers. It was a depressing thought.

❧

Philip Wilder paused at the curb, looked both ways, then dashed across the street to his waiting motorcycle. "Hello, sweetheart," he greeted, running his hand along the sleek curve of the gas tank before popping open the small trunk and retrieving the cobalt blue helmet—the same shocking color as the cycle itself. He loved the bright blue balanced with the abundance of chrome that decorated the classic cycle. The bike was his pride and joy—and he treated it like the child he would likely never have.

Echoes from the meeting on the eighth floor of Branson Building replayed in his mind. The lawyer's voice explaining, "The account is unavailable, Philip. No explanation from the bank. I'll keep trying. If something changes, I'll be in touch." In the meantime, how would Philip pay the bills and keep his business running? He had another month's expenses squirreled away, but after that. . . His heart beat erratically as he considered the number of people relying on him.

God, You have a plan. Hope You'll reveal it to me in time. So much is riding on it. Strapping on his helmet, he glanced toward the building in time to see his elevator mate exit. He watched her, observing how her head hung low, her shoulders slumped as if carrying a weight too heavy to bear. He wondered whom she had been visiting. Whoever it was must have given her some bad news. *Bad News Branson Building*, he thought with a measure of disdain. Then he shook his head, determined to find a positive on which to focus.

Pretty girl, he acknowledged. But he'd thought that when he'd seen the arrangement of pictures on the corner of Darin Brooks's desk. Unpretentious, but attractive—wholesome. That appealed to him. He considered calling her name, giving her a wave, but then he wrapped the errant hand around the handlebar of the cycle to keep from giving in to that urge. What was he thinking, encouraging contact with Marin Brooks? Despite her despondent appearance right now, she'd no doubt be smiling and laughing soon—Darin Brooks would see to that. The man obviously idolized his daughter. A girl like that had the world by the tail—she surely wouldn't be interested in someone like him. He'd discovered long ago that his life calling didn't appeal to most folks. No, it was best to put aside his desire for a family. His family would be the workers at New Beginnings. They were about all the responsibility one man could handle.

His helmet secured, he swung his leg over the bike. The engine revved to life with a thrust of his foot against the kick start. As he backed out of his parking space, he sent a glance skyward and spoke aloud. "Okay, God, remember what I said. I need a plan—and quick. Start thinking, and when You've got it worked out, fill me in. Thanks."

two

Marin, I am going to sort my job now." John stood in the doorway of their father's den. He refused to step over the threshold despite Marin's invitation.

Marin admitted she felt like an interloper sitting in Dad's soft, black leather executive chair behind the massive antique banker's desk with a towering credenza behind her. Dad had always looked so at home in this setting—Marin probably looked ridiculous, dwarfed by the size of the furnishings. But she needed to become accustomed to the feel of sitting in Dad's chair. She needed to learn to fill his shoes.

"Your job?" Then Marin remembered. "Oh, you're going to sort the bottles and cans."

John nodded, his face shining. "Yes. It is my job. I will do it now for Mom." His chin dropped, the sunny expression clouding over. In slow motion he shook his head, his thin hair flopping across his forehead. "No. I will not do it for Mom. Not anymore. I will do it for you, Marin."

Marin's heart turned over in her chest. John was transferring his affection for their mother to her—accepting her as his caretaker. She found it touching. And scary. "Thank you." Her voice sounded tight. She swallowed and gave her brightest smile. "Do you need any extra bags?"

"I will find them. You stay here." John waved his stubby hand at her and disappeared, his slogging steps fading away as he made his way to the kitchen.

Marin sat and listened to the noises—cans clinking, water running, the creak of a milk carton being crushed. John fully understood the recycling. She smiled. He took such pride in it. The telephone rang, and she snatched it up. "Hello?"

"Marin? This is Lenore."

Marin stifled a sigh and slumped back into the chair. Not again. "Aunt Lenore. What can I do for you?"

"Not a thing. But I can do something for you." Lenore's authoritative voice boomed through the lines. "I did some calling today. Did you know there's a facility in Harper that takes Down's syndrome people?"

Marin felt heat building. "Aunt Lenore, you know Mother never liked you to refer to John as a 'Down's syndrome person.' He's a person first. He simply has a disability."

"Yes, a disability that consumed your mother's life." Her aunt's tone was hard, unforgiving. "And now you're going to carry on in her stead. Well, young woman, I will not stand by and see another life ruined by that—"

"Stop!" Marin wished she could throw the phone across the room. She took a deep breath, praying silently for control before speaking again. "Aunt Lenore, I know you love me, and I know you think you're doing what's best for me, but you aren't helping me at all by trying to shuffle John off to some institution where he'd die of loneliness. If you really want to help me, why don't you offer to take John for a couple of afternoons each week? I'm going to have to make some sort of day-care arrangements for him. If he were with you, at least he'd be with family part of the time." The silence at the other end was deafening.

"Aunt Lenore?" Finally her aunt's voice came, breathless and full of disbelief. "You want me to take—? Marin, you must be kidding."

Marin released a brief, humorless snort. "Yes, I suppose I am. That wouldn't work at all, would it? You probably don't even recycle."

"What?"

With a sigh Marin shook her head. "Never mind. Listen—I appreciate your checking in, but I really must run. I'm trying to go through Dad's accounts and see which have precedence.

I'll talk to you later, okay?" She didn't give her aunt a chance to reply. "Good-bye." She placed the phone back in its cradle then sat staring at the telephone for several minutes, certain it would ring again. When it didn't, she heaved a sigh of relief and went back to her file. But just as she got focused, John reappeared in the doorway.

"Marin? I am all done." In his excitement he expressed himself with sign language in addition to verbal words. "I put the bags in the gaw–gaw—" Impatiently he chopped out the sign for *garage*, unwilling to form the tricky *r* in the word.

"Good," Marin praised him, surprised by how much her voice sounded like her mother's. "Thank you."

John beamed, wringing his short fingers together. "I will take my bath now. And then I will want my toast."

Marin nodded, familiar with his nighttime routine. "Fine. You take your bath. And when you're in your pajamas, come and get me, and we'll have toast together."

John wagged his head up and down, smiling. "Yes. Together we will have toast." He disappeared from view once more, and before long the spatter of water against the porcelain tub could be heard, followed by John's cheerful, off-tune singing.

Marin leaned her chin in her hand, listening, a fond smile tugging at her lips. She could almost hear her mother sighing, "Dear John. . ." Mother had always stood outside the bathroom door and listened as John sang. Somewhere he'd heard that people sang in the shower. He hated showers—the splash of water in his face upset him—but he loved his bath and would always sing at the top of his lungs as he scrubbed himself clean.

"Dear John. . ." Mom would sigh as she stood in his doorway and watched him sleep. "Dear John. . ." with pride shining in her eyes when he learned something new, like tying his shoes at age nine.

"Dear John. . ." Marin heard herself release the words, and a bubble of sadness welled in her chest. Had her mother ever stood outside Marin's room, watching her sleep, murmuring,

"Dear Marin. . ."? How Mother had loved John! Marin could never remember a time her mother had been impatient with John. Always she had been giving, tender, full of wisdom. She seemed to know instinctively what John needed and never hesitated to meet his needs. At times Marin had envied their relationship—she never felt as if she mattered as much to Mom as John did.

At the same time she had always wondered if Dad truly loved John or was simply resigned to taking care of him. Her father had never been brusque or uncaring with John, but his relationship had been somehow distant. Sometimes she'd seen her father sit and watch John with a pained expression on his face. She wished now she had asked him what he had been thinking as he silently watched his only son.

Marin dropped her gaze to the file on her father's desk. Dad had been meticulous in his record keeping. It would be easy for her to step in where he had left off. But it would take time to acclimate to the office, to get to know the staff, to discover the needs of her clients. Time she didn't have unless she found someone to care for John.

The thought worried her. Mom had never wanted John to be with strangers. But unless a relative stepped forward and offered to keep him, Marin would have no choice. Just during the days, though, she told herself. Never what Aunt Lenore suggested—an institution or home where other people with handicaps were shuttled away from their families. Mom would turn over in her grave, and Marin would never be able to live with the guilt of sending John away. She sighed again. "Tomorrow I'll make some calls—maybe Aunt Chris will have some suggestions." Dad's sister was much less abrasive than Mom's sister.

"Toast now, Marin!" John stood in the doorway in his pajamas, his wet hair slicked down, a huge grin on his face.

As always, the sight of John in his pajamas gave Marin a start. His behavior was so childlike that it seemed odd to see him in men's two-piece pajamas and a plaid robe. Shouldn't he be wearing flannels with trains or puppy dogs printed on the fabric? Marin lifted herself from the chair and met John in the doorway, linking arms with him.

"Toast," she agreed. "With butter and sugar, right?"

"Butter and sugar, right." John nodded, easily pleased.

Marin hoped the accommodations she found for John's daytime hours would please him as readily as the promise of buttered toast with a sprinkle of sugar.

Because she didn't know what else to do with him, on Wednesday morning of the first week following her parents' deaths, Marin loaded John in her car and took him with her to Brooks Advertising. Before entering the building, she gave him a bright smile. "Okay, here's the office. I know you've been here before, right? Remember the people here are working, so we can't stop and talk to everyone we see. But you can wave and say hi, okay?"

John gave her one of his looks—squinty eyes, pursed lips, chin pulled down until it doubled. "I am not stupid, Marin. I know I cannot bother people who are working."

Marin squeezed his hand. "I know you're not stupid. I'm sorry if I sounded like I thought you were. I'm just a little nervous."

John's expression changed to one of surprise. "You are nervous, Marin?" His hands formed the sign for *nervous* as he spoke.

Marin nodded, nibbling at her lower lip. "Yes, I am." But she didn't expand on the reason. Would Dad's employees accept her leadership, or would they see her as the boss's little girl trying to be a big shot? She wanted Dad's business to continue being the success he had made it—and she would need their help. Would her planned speech help them see how much she needed their cooperation without making her sound like an inexperienced kid?

Marin nearly snorted. Had she ever been a kid, in the true sense? Not really.

"Are we going in, Marin?"

Marin gave a start, having drifted away in thought. She shot a glance at John, waking up, then nodded. "Yes. Let's go."

She swung open her car door and John followed suit, ambling around the hood of the car with his hand extended. She knew what he wanted. Obligingly she handed him the automatic lock and let him push the button.

At the "beep" indicating the doors were locked, he beamed. "All is safe!"

Marin smiled, wishing her emotions could be so easily safeguarded. She took the keys back and dropped them into her purse then led John into the offices. Brooks Advertising was located in the older part of downtown Petersburg, Kansas, and still retained the appearance of its 1920s beginning. Marin liked the sense of stability the red brick building with its ornate plaster scrolls and window casings projected.

Inside, hardwood floors shone with a high polish, and the twelve-foot ceiling bore pressed tin panels. The plaster walls were painted a soft mauve above beaded wainscoting. A beautiful border that resembled a burgundy swag separated the paneling from the painted wall. The soft colors were at once welcoming and relaxing. Dad had done a great job of maintaining the tradition of the structure without sacrificing today's style.

John immediately waved to the receptionist, Crystal Brown, and Crystal gave a hesitant wave in return. Marin had learned early to detect when someone was uncomfortable with John's disability. Crystal tried to hide it, but her frozen smile and stiff gestures gave her away.

"Is everyone in the meeting room?" Marin asked, pausing at Crystal's desk, which was a 1920s soda counter reconstructed to meet the needs of a secretary.

"Yes, all in and accounted for, Miss Brooks." Crystal's gaze darted to John as if worried he would do something unusual and she might miss it.

"Great. I'll talk to you later." Marin turned to John. "John, do you want to sit out here and look at the magazines? I'll be back in a few minutes."

John nodded and padded to the reception area where a large oval rug held a circle of upholstered chairs and a low table arranged neatly with a variety of magazines. He picked one up and held it out to Marin with a huge smile. "Cars, Marin! I will look at the one about cars!"

Marin gave him the thumbs-up sign. "Great choice. Back soon." She turned and clicked her way to the meeting room, her heart rate increasing with every step. Before entering the room, she ran her hands over the slim skirt of her jade green suit and touched the collar of her white blouse. Dad had always dressed to the hilt when coming to the office, and Marin had tried to emulate his appearance in her feminine way. "The clothes make the man," Dad had always said. Marin hoped her professional appearance would help hide her inner nervousness.

Swinging the paneled door open, she offered a big smile to the four employees seated at the round meeting table. Dad had insisted on a round table to make everyone feel equal—just like King Arthur's round table. One seat was open—Dad's. Marin swallowed a bubble of sorrow as she moved to that chair and rested her hands on its high back.

"Good morning, everyone," she greeted them, letting her gaze rove around the group, offering a smile to each person. They smiled and offered greetings in return, but she could sense their unease, as if waiting for a shoe to drop.

"First of all, I want to thank all of you for being so dedicated to my father in the years you've worked with him. He always spoke highly of his staff, he considered you his friends as well as his employees, and I know he'd be pleased you were all here, ready to continue with his business." Marin paused, fighting the urge to cry. She would not cry! She had to be strong! Swallowing, she forced a smile she didn't feel.

Taking advantage of a moment to gain control, she pulled out Dad's chair and gingerly slid into the wooden seat. Folding her hands on the edge of the table, she continued. "I'm sure you have lots of questions about where the company will go from here. I assure you, I have some, too!" She laughed lightly and felt relief when answering smiles broke across their faces. "But I do know one thing—Dad's company will continue just as he would intend it. Brooks Advertising has built a reputation of integrity and quality. That will not change. The only difference is essentially a consonant change in the ownership—from Darin to Marin. It's what Dad wanted, and I will do my best to be the kind of leader my dad was—fair, approachable, and knowledgeable."

The oldest of the employees, Dick Ross, raised his hand. "Miss Brooks—Marin—I appreciate your statement and your desire to keep the business running. But"—he glanced around the table, and Marin got the impression whatever he was about to say had been discussed between the employees before she got here—"with all due respect, your father had been in this business for years. You are newly graduated from college without experience in running a business. Are you sure you are up to the challenge?"

Marin felt the familiar swell of guilt that came with the mention of her graduation. Resolutely she pushed it aside to ask in an even tone, "Up to the challenge? I believe so, Dick." She intentionally used the man's first name, knowing her father would have addressed him in that manner. "I realize you haven't seen me in these offices a great deal, but Dad and I often conferred in his office at home. He kept me up-to-date on his accounts, explained why he chose one design over another, brainstormed with me. . . . He made me a part of Brooks Advertising because he knew one day I would *be* Brooks Advertising."

A sad smile tugged at the corners of her lips. "Of course, our hope was we would work together for several years before he handed over the reins. But that wasn't to be. So I'm going to make the best of our current situation."

She paused, unlinking her fingers to place her palms flat against the thick oak table top, gathering strength from the solid surface at which her father's hands had so often rested. "But I can't do it alone. I will depend on each of you"—she let her gaze rest on Dick's face the longest—"to assist me in this transition. Please communicate with me, keep me abreast of what your clients want, attend the morning meetings, just as you always did with Dad. Be patient with me as I learn to fill Dad's shoes. We all know they are big shoes to fill."

Tears threatened, but she blinked, keeping them at bay. Tears had no place here. "I will do my best, but this company has always been a group effort—Dad's name is in the title, but all of you are essential if Brooks Advertising is going to function the way it has for the past twenty years. I hope your commitment to the company will remain strong."

"You can count on me, Marin," Randall Stucky inserted, his blue eyes meeting her gaze head on. "I had a great deal of respect for Darin Brooks. He gave me my first chance to prove myself in advertising. I won't let him down."

Marin smiled warmly. "Thanks, Randall. I appreciate that."

"You said we'd be having our morning meetings, just as Darin led them," Hannah Dutton said.

Marin nodded in her direction. "Yes, that's my intention."

Hannah flushed slightly but raised her chin and continued. "Your father always began our morning meetings with a word of prayer. Will that be a tradition you follow, Marin?"

Marin froze momentarily, unsure how to answer. She knew Dad had been a firm believer in prayer. He'd prayed with her often at home. Marin had accepted Jesus into her heart as a little girl as a result of her parents' gentle guidance. But prayer had been Dad's arena—he was the spiritual leader in the home. She hadn't considered assuming that role. It left her frightened and uncertain.

Hannah and the others waited for an answer. She had to say something. She opened her mouth and heard herself admitting, "To be honest, I hadn't processed that far. I've never seen myself in that kind of leadership position." She squared her shoulders. "But it was important to Dad to build this company on the Bible and on the premises of his faith, so I will continue in Dad's tradition there, as well."

The others nodded as Marin's throat tightened. *Help me do this, God!* Marin had prayed that simple prayer dozens of times since the phone call telling her of the accident. *Help me do this, God*, as she'd planned her parents' funeral. *Help me do this, God*, as she'd dealt with Aunt Lenore's pressure. *Help me do this, God*, now as she bowed her head to offer a prayer.

"Heavenly Father. . ." Marin heard the quaver in her voice as emotion rose. Tears stung behind her closed lids. *Help me do this, God.* "We come before You today with heavy hearts because someone we cared for—someone we've depended on—is gone. But, God, we are all aware of what Dad wanted when he built Brooks Advertising. He wanted to build a company that reflected Your face to every person who walked through the doors. Help us continue Dad's company the way he intended. Give us the knowledge and wisdom to meet the needs of the people who call upon our services. Help us bond as a group; help us learn to work together without Dad's gentle leading. Help me be the best leader I can be. Bless each of these employees seated around this table—thank You for their dedication to You and to Dad. Thank You for being here with us. Let us feel Your comforting presence as we move forward. In Jesus' name we pray, amen."

Marin raised her head to find a glimmer of tears in the eyes of some of the people seated around the table. She offered a quavering smile. "Thank you. I won't be able to stay today, but I'll try to be back tomorrow—I hope for the entire day—and we'll have a chance to get caught up on everyone's projects. In the meantime, I know I can trust you to finish the work you were doing before Dad's. . .death." It still hurt to say the word.

Everyone stood and filed out, stopping to touch Marin's shoulder or shake her hand, to offer another word of condolence or a "welcome" message. Dick was the last to leave, and he paused, his head down, obviously deciding how to approach whatever was on his mind. Marin waited patiently.

"Marin," he finally said, his gaze averted, "I've been with your dad a long time, and I loved him like a brother. I'll be honest—I'm concerned about how things will go now. You're young. I know you mean well, and I'm sure there's plenty of Darin in you to give starch to your spine, but you're going to be carrying a mighty load keeping up with the responsibility of this company as well as your. . .responsibility. . .at home."

Marin felt warmth climb her cheeks. John again. For a moment she wished she could dive back into the elevator of Branson Building with the tall stranger, the one person who'd spoken to her in the past several days and not mentioned her brother.

Dick's face was set in a grim expression, but Marin could see sympathy in his eyes. "Darin had Mary to take care of home. Your name might be a combination of Darin and Mary, but you can't be both people, Marin. No one could be both people—it's too much. As harsh as it sounds, you're going to have to do something with John."

At that moment Marin heard a movement at the door, and she looked over her shoulder. John had opened the door a crack and was peeking in, one hazel eye crinkled with smile lines. Without effort she smiled back. "I'll be there in just a minute, John." The door closed.

She turned back to Dick. "I know what you're saying, but there is no way I can do what you're suggesting. You're right that my name is a combination of my parents'—and each of them bestowed in me the best of their hearts. Mom loved John with everything she had. Dad took care of him by providing financially. They would never forgive me if I didn't continue caring for him with the same dedication. Somehow I will make this work. I promise you that."

Dick shook his head, his glasses reflecting the overhead light and hiding his eyes from view. "I admire your spunk, Marin—reminds me of Darin—but I still think you're biting off more than you can chew."

"Then pray for me," Marin challenged, surprised at her boldness. She heard a giggle from behind the door. She added in a grim tone, "I'm going to need all the prayers I can get."

three

Marin slammed down the phone and clasped the hair at her temples. She hadn't realized it would be so difficult to find day-care arrangements for John. Every place she'd located in the yellow pages had a waiting list. If she heard, "If you had called six months ago. . ." one more time, she might scream. If she'd known six months ago that her parents would be dead and she would be the sole provider for her brother, maybe she would have called! The statement was ludicrous, given her circumstances. Marin fought the urge to lay her head on the desk and bawl.

It was getting late, but maybe she could make one more call. She heaved a huge sigh then looked in the phone book again. The next listing was New Beginnings. Although the information was scanty, she resolutely punched in the numbers and waited for an answer.

On the third ring she heard the receiver being lifted. "Hello, New Beginnings!" The masculine voice seemed vaguely familiar.

"Yes, I'm seeking a day-care arrangement for my brother who has Down's syndrome." Marin began her spiel, feeling as if she could recite the words by rote. "He is thirty-one years old, and—"

"What level?"

Marin stopped, confused. "Excuse me?"

The voice at the other end laughed. "I'm sorry. Let me rephrase that. You said your brother has Down's syndrome, right?"

"Yes."

"Okay. So is his disjunction, mosaicism, or translocation?"

Marin rubbed her chin. "I—I'm not sure."

"Well, then, don't worry about it. But levels of the retardation seem to vary among the different types, so knowing that can help me place him initially."

Marin's heart lifted at the end of his statement. "You mean, you might be able to provide day-care services for my brother?"

Another low chuckle was emitted, and Marin was sure she'd heard that sound before. "Well, I gotta tell you—this isn't exactly a day care. This is a job placement service."

Marin's heart fell. Job placement? "I'm sorry. I didn't realize. . . . I don't think you'll be able to help me after all." Marin started to hang up, but she heard a frantic voice calling from the telephone receiver.

"Wait! Wait!"

She placed the receiver against her ear. Impatience with her helplessness and pressure of her need came through clearly in her tone. "What? My brother is thirty-one years old, and he's not been out of our house for more than outings. Job placement is ridiculous. It would never work. I appreciate your time, but—"

"Now just hold on." The voice took on an authoritative tone. "You say your brother has never been out of the house, except for outings, in thirty years?"

Marin flumped back in the chair and crossed her legs. "That's right."

"So what has he been doing all that time?"

Marin blinked. Doing? "Well, he's been with my mom. Helping her, I guess. I've been away at college, so I really am not sure how he's spent his days." Marin turned her ear to the living room, where the stereo suddenly came on full blast. Thumping noises told her John was dancing. She'd need to get off the telephone soon.

"And he isn't helping her anymore?"

Marin pinched the bridge of her nose. "No. My mom was

killed in an accident a little over a week ago. So I need to find someone to take care of John while I'm at work."

"Oh." The voice carried a hint of sympathy now. "I see. And your dad can't help?"

Marin swallowed hard. It was so difficult to go over this, especially with a stranger. "He and Mom were together in the accident. Neither survived."

"Hey, I'm sorry." Marin could tell by the gentle tone he meant it. "You've really inherited a responsibility, haven't you?" She didn't reply, just held the phone tight against her head, relishing the understanding that came through the phone line. "Listen—I'd like to help you out, but—"

Marin suspected she knew where this was going. Before someone else could disappoint her, she cut in. "I thank you for your time and concern, but it's obvious to me that my brother and your work program are not a good match. Good-bye." She hung up before he could respond.

She sat at the desk, staring at the phone book. The only other listing was a group home in nearby Garden City—and Marin didn't want to put John in a group home. She gave in to the earlier urge and let her forehead rest on the phone book while tears welled again. *Oh, please help me, God. What am I going to do?*

❧

Philip traced over the telephone number he'd recorded from the caller ID. Since it wasn't in his phone's memory bank, he had no idea to whom he had just been speaking, but his heart ached for the hopelessness he'd heard in the young woman's voice. He didn't know if he'd be able to help her—if the brother had been at home with the mother, without schooling, for thirty years, it was possible it was too late.

In his years of working with people with disabilities Philip had learned that much rested on the formative years. A twenty-point increase in IQ could be made if the parents simply exposed the child to the same activities as one would do with a "normal" child. *If there is such a thing*, he thought with a brief laugh.

He'd found that when a child with disabilities came into a family, the family often rallied around to protect the child. Not that he could blame them. Philip knew valid reasons existed for forming a protective barrier. But when it was carried to the extreme, the protective barrier could hinder learning. But if the mother of this man had sent him to school, if he had learned basic self-help skills, then there was a good possibility Philip could work with him. He wanted to try.

He was certain the woman wouldn't call again. She'd sounded as if she was at the end of her rope, however, and he wished he'd had the foresight to ask her name before she hung up. He ran the pencil lead over the final digit, darkening it more than the other six numbers in the telephone number. So she wouldn't call him. Didn't mean he wouldn't call her. But he'd really like a name to go with the voice before he spoke to her again.

Suddenly an idea struck. "Hey! Thanks, God!" he said, giving the credit to the One he was sure planted the thought. Flipping open his telephone directory, he began scanning the list of numbers.

❧

Marin turned off John's light and whispered, " 'Night, John. Sleep tight."

" 'Night, Marin," came his sleepy voice in return. No doubt worn out from his dance session, he should sleep well tonight.

She closed his door and took one step toward her bedroom when the telephone rang. She frowned. Who would be calling at ten o'clock? She sighed. She hoped it wasn't Aunt Lenore. A glance at the caller ID confirmed it wasn't, but she didn't recognize the number. For a moment Marin hesitated. But she was afraid the incessant ring would bother John, so at the fourth ring she snatched it up.

"Hello?"

"Is this Marin Brooks?"

For a reason she didn't understand, Marin's heart began to pound. "Yes. To whom am I speaking?"

"Philip Wilder—New Beginnings."

It took Marin a moment before a picture of the man from Branson Building's elevator—his tall stature, warm smile, and relaxed apparel—appeared in her memory. It gave her an odd feeling, but now she understood why his voice had seemed familiar.

"Listen, Marin—I'm so sorry about your parents. I didn't know. When I talked to you on the elevator and told you to tell your dad. . ." He paused, the silence heavy. His voice sounded husky as he finished quietly, "I wish I'd known."

"It's okay." Marin finally was able to form words. "How did you know it was me who called?"

Another pause. Then, almost shyly, his voice came again. "Well, I had your number—it came through on caller ID. So I got out the phone book and started hunting. Only 3,500 names—not that big of a deal." That low, throaty chuckle sounded again; only this time it held a hint of self-consciousness. "But it sure helped that you're in the Bs or it would've taken a lot longer."

Marin dropped onto the couch, the phone still pressed to her ear. He had gone through the telephone book? "But why?"

"You hung up on me before I could finish what I was saying," he said. "I know we aren't a day-care facility, but we still might be able to help your brother. What did you say his name is?"

"John," Marin answered automatically. "His name is John. But as I told you, he's never been involved in any kind of employment. I can't imagine he'd be of any use to you there."

"You'd be surprised. So many people look at the disabled, and all they see is a disability. I like to see the ability in the person."

Marin digested this. She liked the way it sounded.

Philip continued. "Tell me about your brother. What are the things he enjoys?"

Immediately Marin pictured John dancing around the room—swinging his hips and snapping his fingers to a Steven Curtis Chapman CD. She smiled. "He likes music. He enjoys dancing, although he isn't very good at it by most standards. Different sounds seem to capture his attention—rings, beeps, squawks. He has a fascination with noises. I have to watch him. If an appliance makes an unusual sound, he'll take it apart to see what's doing it."

A light chuckle came through the line. "What else? Does he have chores around the house?"

"Chores?" Marin shrugged. "Well, yes, I suppose so. He makes his own bed, keeps his bathroom clean, clears the table after dinner. And his job is recycling."

"Job? You said he didn't leave the house."

Marin heard his confusion. A light laugh escaped her lips—the first since her parents' death. Amazing how good it felt to release it. "He calls it his job. Actually he rinses all the recyclable items and sorts them in the garage for pickup."

"He categorizes them?"

Marin felt surprised by the enthusiasm she heard in his tone. "Yes. Puts the plastics together, the glass, so on. It isn't complicated."

"No, but what you're telling me is that John is able to sort items—categorize them according to common characteristics and put them away without guidance."

"That's what I'm telling you." Marin still could not see any significance in what she had shared, but it was obvious that Philip was excited by her words.

"That's wonderful. Did John go to school?"

Marin leaned back into the cushions of the couch and hugged a throw pillow to her. Her comfortable position invited a lengthier conversation. "Yes. He attended special education classes."

"EMH or TMH?"

"EMH, I believe. I can't be sure. John is eight years older than I am, so I was still in elementary school when he finished his education."

"Marin, if John attended classes for the educable mentally handicapped, then he definitely qualifies for job placement through New Beginnings."

Marin sat up straight. "You're kidding? On the basis of sorting recyclables?"

Philip laughed. "I do have some placements for the trainable mentally handicapped, but most are for EMH. I could work with John here at New Beginnings and eventually place him at any number of locations—a school to do custodial work or a fast-food restaurant clearing tables and mopping up. Maybe even—"

"Whoa, hold on!" Marin threw the pillow aside. This was going too fast. "You want John to be in a regular work place—not at wherever you're located, which I assume is a protected environment, but out where he'll encounter all kinds of people."

"That's exactly what I shoot for."

"Then we're not interested." She stood, the pressure building in her chest again. She had hoped—but, no, John couldn't handle it. Marin couldn't handle it if something happened to him out there.

"But why not?" Philip didn't sound angry, just curious.

Marin sighed. "Philip, it isn't that I don't appreciate your taking the time to track me down and tell me a little more about your program. But you don't understand my needs. All I need is a place for John to 'hang out' while I'm at work—a safe place for him to spend the day. So I'm sorry, but I'm going to have to look elsewhere."

"There is no elsewhere, Marin. Not unless you want him in an institution."

A stab of pain struck. That's exactly what she wanted to

avoid. Anger billowed, and she took her frustration out on the man at the other end of the telephone line. "Why do you have to be so negative?"

"I'm not being negative. I'm only telling you the truth. There are basically two options: put the disabled away where we don't have to see them or acknowledge their presence, or somehow integrate them with our world. I prefer the latter. I thought you did, too. After all, you called me looking for help."

"I do need help! But I don't want John to be hurt!"

"Good. That means we have the same goal."

His calm reply deflated Marin's anger. Why was she yelling at this man who was only trying to offer her a solution to her problem? When she didn't say anything in response, he began speaking again in a hushed tone that invited complete attention.

"Listen, Marin. I think I told you your dad did some advertising brochures for me. In our conversation I got the impression he was a Christian. Am I right?"

"Yes. Dad was a strong Christian."

"And are you?"

Marin considered his question. She had accepted Christ, but she didn't see herself as the spiritual giant she perceived her parents to be. Still, there was no other accurate answer. "Yes."

"Then you believe God has a plan for each life, don't you? I believe that, too. God put a seed in my heart a long time ago, when I was still a boy. Something. . .happened. . . to make me see a need existed for people with disabilities and people without disabilities to learn to work together and accept one another. That seed coming to fruit is New Beginnings. I opened it four years ago to help people like your brother find a way to feel as if they belong in society. With God's help lives have been changed."

Marin clutched the telephone receiver with both hands.

"That's all very well and good—and I admire your stand—but I'm still not sure it's a good fit for John." She swallowed hard, lowering her voice to a whisper. "Philip, we've always kept John away from public places. Not completely, of course—he's attended church with the family, and he goes out for dinner or shopping. But whenever he's gone out, he's been with my parents—never by himself. Mom didn't trust people with him. John is so open to everyone, so loving, that he's a prime target for cruel jokes. I don't think my mother would approve of my placing him in a program that would intentionally put him in the public eye."

"I do understand your concern, Marin." Philip's voice held compassion. "Believe me, I have the same concerns. That's why this program is carefully monitored. I'd be happy to give you some names of families who have made use of New Beginnings and are glad they did."

She wavered. "I don't know. . . ."

His voice came again, strong in his conviction. "Marin, I don't think it was an accident that you and I met in the elevator at Branson Building. And I don't think it was an accident that I happened to be in the building three hours later than my normal schedule, making it possible for you to talk to me rather than my answering machine when you called here tonight. New Beginnings is here to help you, but New Beginnings is useless unless people like you trust me enough to *let* me help them."

Marin sighed, sitting back down. She rested her chin on her hand. The idea of John in a public workplace, where people might laugh and point and—she shivered—do worse things, did not set comfortably. But Philip was a good salesman. He had her thinking. She hedged. "Could we visit? Maybe see what you do?"

"Sure!" She could almost feel Philip's smile come through the line. "That would be great. Would nine o'clock tomorrow morning work for you?"

Marin considered this. She had intended to go to the office tomorrow, to become familiar with the routine there. But until she found a place for John she wouldn't be able to go to work anyway. They'd have to go another couple of days without her. "Yes. I can make that work."

"Wonderful! Do you have the address?"

"Yes, it's in the phone book."

"Good. I'll see you then. And, Marin?"

The way he spoke her name left her feeling tingly under her skin. "Yes?"

"Don't coach John before you come. Let him be himself."

Marin frowned. Didn't she always let John be himself? "Okay."

"I'll see you and John tomorrow. Sleep well, Marin." The phone line went dead.

Marin sat for a moment, staring at the buzzing receiver. Then she carefully placed it in the cradle. *Sleep well, Marin,* he had said. He'd sounded like a friend—like someone who cared. Marin needed all the friends she could get right now. She hoped this Philip Wilder proved to be as good as he sounded.

four

Philip hung up the phone then leaned back in his squeaky, secondhand desk chair, propped his heels on the edge of the scarred desk, and linked his fingers behind his head. He smiled, remembering the attractive girl from the elevator. Then the smile drooped as he recalled her bearing when she left Branson Building as well as her defeated tone on the telephone. *She must feel as if she's carrying the weight of the world right now,* he mused, *losing both of her parents and having to assume so much responsibility.*

Philip understood the weight of responsibility. He ignored the jumble of papers on his metal desk, keeping his eyes aimed toward the ceiling. He'd stared at the figures long enough earlier in the evening to know if something didn't change quickly, New Beginnings would be just a memory in a very short time. Maybe he was foolish, bringing in new clients when the fate of New Beginnings was so uncertain. What else could he do, though, but trust that somehow things would work out? His Bible told him all things worked for good to those who were called according to God's purpose. Wasn't he serving God's purpose by reaching out to those who were often rejected? He knew without a doubt New Beginnings was God's plan for his life.

His thoughts drifted back a dozen years, to that beautiful April afternoon that had turned suddenly ugly—the afternoon when the difference between disabled and non-disabled had become all too clear. He shook his head, pushing away the memory. It stung even after all this time. The guilt still weighed on him like a millstone around his neck. He had to keep New Beginnings running—he had to do now what he hadn't done then.

Bringing his clasped hands to his chest, he bowed his head and prayed—asked for forgiveness again. Asked God to remove the burden of guilt. From there he offered a prayer for Marin's peace then asked God to help him find the best way to help this young woman and her brother. Each time he helped a person with a disability find a way to belong in society, it helped appease his guilt.

His prayer finished, he kept his eyes closed and thought back to the day almost five years ago when he'd visited Brooks Advertising with the purpose of putting together some brochures that would let people know what New Beginnings was all about. Not once had Darin Brooks mentioned he had a son who could benefit from the services New Beginnings offered. The only hint—and it hadn't carried real significance until now—the man had someone close to him who was disabled was the fact that, when Philip went to pay, Mr. Brooks had refused to take his money.

"No, son," he'd said, "I choose two accounts each year to do pro bono. I'd appreciate it if you'd accept being one of them."

Philip had been thrilled. Relying on donations and a small government stipend to get the services up and running, the money he'd set aside for brochures could be used a dozen different ways. He'd accepted Mr. Brooks's kind offer with a lump in his throat.

Philip rocked his chair, pressing his memory. Funny, when Philip had been in Darin Brooks's office, he had seen only pictures of Marin, not of John. Philip wondered about that now. Was the man ashamed of his son, or was he afraid of people's reaction to his having a handicapped child? Philip would never know for sure since the man was now gone. He hoped John hadn't been kept hidden away from people as much as Marin had implied. At thirty-one, it would be hard to change him if he'd never had social interaction. Not impossible, but hard. And Philip was running out of time.

Scowling, he dropped his feet with a thump against the concrete floor and buried his face in his hands. He wished he'd hear from the lawyer to know whether or not New Beginnings would be able to continue. There were so many needy people, and Philip believed from the depth of his soul that God had led him to help. He *had* to help—his own personal worth depended on it. "I'm in need of a miracle here, God," Philip said, speaking to the high, echoing ceiling. "You're the God of miracles. You've always met my needs in the past. Have no reason to doubt You now. But I do wish You'd hurry up a bit, because I have to admit, I'm starting to get nervous."

❧

The cowbell hanging above the metal door clanged loudly, signaling the arrival of guests. Philip lifted his gaze from the mop, which Anita, one of his clients, was attempting to wring, and his heart leaped into his throat.

Sunlight slipped in behind the couple framed in the doorway, creating a halo of the woman's shining blond hair. She looked fragile next to the bulky build of the man who stood next to her—obviously her brother, John—but Philip knew that *fragile* wasn't a word one would use to describe Marin Brooks. The young woman had a great deal of inner strength—he was certain of that. John stood with shoulders hunched forward, his almond-shaped eyes warily glancing right and left, his stubby hands clasped against his chest. The pose didn't inspire Philip's confidence.

"Anita, I'll be right back," he said, touching the woman's shoulder. He waited for her nod of acknowledgment before jogging across the floor to greet Marin and John Brooks officially. "Marin, you made it." He stuck out his hand, and she placed her small hand within his.

Her narrow fingers with neatly manicured nails rested there for the length of two slight pumps before she withdrew them. She didn't return his smile. "Yes, we're here. Philip, this is my brother, John."

Philip turned his brightest smile on the man who stood only a couple of inches taller than his sister. John's thin blond hair was neatly combed, his clothing unrumpled, with the red and blue polo shirt tucked into his jeans. White leather sneakers covered his feet. It pleased Philip that John was attired like any other "normal" person. Some families didn't see fit to dress their children with handicaps as neatly as their non-handicapped children. The unkempt appearance only added to society's disdain.

"It's nice to meet you, John," Philip said as he extended his hand.

John slowly brought his right hand forward and placed it in Philip's palm. But he didn't grip.

Lesson number one, Philip thought. "Hey, buddy, let me show you something." Philip pulled his hand back and flexed his fingers. "Can you close your fingers like this?"

John tipped his head, examining Philip's hand. He brought up his hand and imitated the movement.

"That's right, just like you're grabbing an ice cream cone or the stick on a corn dog."

John grinned shyly. "I like ice cream." He pronounced each word carefully.

Philip could easily understand the man's speech. That was a plus. Philip winked. "Me, too, buddy." He lowered his hand, offering it again. "Now this time when you take my hand to shake it, pretend you're taking hold of an ice cream cone and give me a firm grasp, okay?"

John wagged his head up and down twice and followed Philip's instruction.

"Now that's a handshake!" Philip praised as John smiled broadly. He gave John a light clap on the shoulder. "Anytime someone wants to shake your hand, you grab firmly, okay? Makes a good impression."

Again John nodded, still smiling. "I will make a good impression, Marin."

"I know you will," Marin confirmed in a warm tone.

Philip let his gaze drift back to Marin. Her eyes appeared as wary as her brother's had been. She wouldn't be as easily won over as John.

"So what do we do here?" Marin lifted her shoulders in a graceful gesture of query. "Do you give us a tour, do we fill out some paperwork. . . ?"

Philip chuckled, pinching his chin between his fingers. "The paperwork can wait, Marin." He noticed John imitated his stance, and he hid a smile. "I'll show you around, but mostly I want to get acquainted with John this morning—find out what he likes to do, what his strengths are. It will help me find the best situation for him."

While Philip spoke, John rocked back on his heels, letting his gaze rove from Philip's head to his toes. Suddenly he burst out, "You have big feet!"

Marin turned bright pink. "John, that isn't very polite."

But Philip laughed and put his foot next to John's. His own brown work boot dwarfed John's leather sneaker. "You're right, John. I do have big feet. I wear a size 14. What size do you wear?"

"Size 8 shoe. Wide." John recited the list in a monotone. "Size 34 pants. Thirty length. Size 16-and-a-half shirt. Sometimes a medium, sometimes a large if it does not have buttons. And 32/34 shorts." John leaned forward and finished in a whisper. "Undershorts. White only. I do not like colored ones."

Marin looked almost purple by now. Philip bit down on the inside of his cheeks to keep from laughing. He liked John already; but he knew if he laughed, Marin might assume he was making fun of her brother. He was also aware that while he found John's candor endearing, it made him an instant target for cruel people. It was best not to encourage him by laughing right now.

"Well, I bet you're great when it's time to go shopping.

You know just what to look for." Philip clamped his hand on John's shoulder. "But you know, buddy—when it comes to undershorts it's okay to keep that size a secret. Most folks are only interested in the clothes they can see you wear on the outside."

John's hazel eyes crinkled as he gave another face-splitting smile. "Okay. I do not wear undershorts on the outside."

"Nope, no one does," Philip agreed. He dropped his hand and turned to Marin, pleased to see her face returning to its normal color. His heart turned over in sympathy. How difficult this situation had to be for her. He wished he could give her a hug of support, but he suspected she would rebuff him. She seemed to keep herself held firmly aloof. That was probably best, too—her sweet face and tenderness toward her brother were already tugging too much at his heartstrings. He couldn't let himself get too involved.

"Would you like to make the rounds, see what others are doing, while I visit a bit more with John?" Philip asked.

Marin's eyes—hazel like her brother's, but without the gold flecks—widened. "Leave John?"

Philip stifled a sigh. This letting-go process was tougher for some than others. He could see that Marin was going to have a difficult time. But she would have to learn, and this was a good place to start. "John will be in shouting distance." He waved his arm. "New Beginnings isn't that large." He felt gratified when she offered a small, self-conscious smile. "Why don't you sit down here"—he pointed to a molded plastic chair—"and read the brochure of all the options for job placement? We'll be back in a few minutes to talk with you. Okay?"

Still appearing somewhat dubious, Marin seated herself in the chair he had indicated and took the brochure from the table beside it. "Okay." Looking at John, she added, "I'll be close by, John. Don't worry."

"I will be okay. You do not worry, Marin."

Philip grinned. John had more spunk than Marin was willing to accept, he'd wager. He threw his arm around John's shoulders. "C'mon, buddy. I've got some people I'd like you to meet."

&

It didn't take long for Marin to read through the brochure—she recognized the Brooks Advertising logo on the back—and she was impressed with what she saw. Philip had done a commendable job of putting together a variety of programs to meet the needs of physically as well as mentally disabled individuals. She still wasn't convinced it was the right type of arrangement for John, but she did have to admit Philip seemed to know what he was doing.

She glanced around the warehouse-type building. Nothing fancy, but everything was clean. People seemed to be divided into four groups, and it was obvious that two of the people in each group were not disabled. They must be the trainers, she decided. With each trainer were no fewer than four people with some sort of disability. Marin didn't watch any group for long—she didn't want to give the impression she was staring. It made her uncomfortable when people stared at John.

Over the years she'd learned to split people into four categories, with varying degrees of each level. First were the gawkers, who openly stared without compunction, either fearful of or fascinated by John. Next were the ignorers. They looked past John as if he didn't exist, talked over or around him, and left Marin wondering if her brother were invisible. The third group—who meant well, at least—were the sweethearts. They spoke to John the way one would a small child. Although it was better than the previous two, it still set Marin's teeth on edge—he was a grown man. Last, the smallest group by far, were the normals. She admired the few normals who were able to treat John like any other person they encountered. Philip was definitely a normal, and she appreciated his warmth and acceptance.

She lifted her gaze toward the high, metal-beamed ceiling.

A large banner hung on the north wall, bearing the Bible verse from Ephesians 2:10—"For we are God's workmanship, created in Christ Jesus to do good works, which God prepared in advance for us to do." She'd never really considered that God had a plan in place for His children in advance. The thought warmed her. Did God have a plan for John, too? Was New Beginnings part of John's plan?

"Marin, guess what?" John's happy voice interrupted Marin's musings. She turned her head to see both John and Philip approaching. John beamed from ear to ear, and Philip seemed pleased, too. "Philip says I am very good at organizing. This is a good thing, Marin."

Marin rose and hugged John when he held out his arms. "That's terrific."

"Hey, John." Philip's voice captured John's attention, and he pulled loose from Marin's hug. "Do you remember the snacks room?"

John nodded, eyes shining. "Yes. A girl named Anita was eating a chocolate chip cookie." He grinned at Marin. "She is pretty."

Marin carefully refrained from showing worry. In many ways John was like any other young man—he recognized a pretty girl and wanted to show attention to her. But in other ways John was different. Marriage and family weren't possibilities, given John's limitations, and Marin didn't want to see him hurt.

Philip threw back his head and laughed. "Ah, yes, buddy, Anita is a pretty lady. And she's nice, too. Would you like to go have a cookie with her while I talk to your sister?"

John turned his eager gaze in Marin's direction. "Could I go have a cookie with Anita, Marin?"

Marin swallowed the lump that rose in her throat. It felt strange to have Philip witness her giving her older brother permission. "Sure. Go ahead. But not too many, huh? Lunch isn't that far off."

John nodded and headed away, his swaying gait emphasized as he hurried toward the break area. Marin watched him until he disappeared behind a six-foot-high partition. She heard his giggles and released a sigh.

A hand descended on her shoulder, and she turned to find Philip watching her with concern in his eyes. "You're going to give yourself wrinkles if you don't quit that scowling," he said in a teasing voice.

Marin took one step sideways, away from the warm hand. "If you had a brother like John, you'd worry, too." Before he could reply, she asked, "Do you think you'll be able to find a place here for him?"

Philip gestured to the plastic chair she'd sat in earlier. After she seated herself again, he yanked another one from beneath a nearby table and sat down close to her knees. "I could find many placements for John. Marin, he's really very bright—high functioning for Down's. He's personable, follows directions easily, and remembers them well enough to repeat them a few minutes later, and he has a desire to be with others." He crossed his arms, giving his shaggy head a slight shake. "I'll be honest. From what you described on the phone last night, I didn't expect him to be easy to work with. Obviously your mom didn't just follow him around and take care of him—she taught him to do for himself. That's great."

"So you'll be able to use him here." Marin leaned forward, her brows pulled down.

"Marin, as I told you before, New Beginnings isn't a day care. Our goal is to place our clients in jobs—and those jobs are out there." He gestured toward the door. "John is a prime candidate for placement."

"No."

The abrupt reply brought Philip's brows into a sharp V. He rested his elbows on his knees and leaned forward, bringing his face close to hers. Lowering his voice, he offered a gentle reprimand. "Loving people means doing what's best for them, even when it's hard. Keeping John cooped up away from people isn't what's best, Marin."

Marin felt anger building. This man didn't know her or her brother. He didn't know the hurt they'd encountered. How could he sit there and tell her what was best for John? She picked up the brochure and held it up. "This says, 'Meeting needs where they exist.' I interpret that to mean you provide a service to families in need of one. The service I need is day care. Can you or can you not provide that for me?"

Philip sat up straight, his mouth set in a grim line. "If it came down to it, I could. I have eight employees who are here everyday, all day, working with clients, preparing them for their placements. John could stay here, helping out with cleaning and participating in the training classes with the others."

"Good."

Philip held up his hand. "*But*. . .that doesn't mean I will."

Marin released a huff of aggravation. "Why not?"

"Because that isn't the goal of New Beginnings. I don't want to keep my clients shut away from the world. I want them to become a valuable part of the world. I want the non-disabled to see them as valuable. That can't happen if they are kept apart from one another."

"I don't want him out there."

Philip shook his head. "You must be the most stubborn mother I've ever worked with." His smile softened the words. Without warning his large hand snaked out to capture her fingers. Although she tensed and tried to pull away, he continued to hold her hand, stroking her knuckles with his thumb.

"Marin, believe me—I understand your concern. There are people who take advantage of those with handicaps—who are even intentionally cruel. But don't you see—the perceptions that people with handicaps are unworthy of fair treatment can never be changed unless a relationship is established between the handicapped and non-handicapped. That's what New Beginnings is all about—bridging the differences that exist between the disabled and non-disabled. John is so friendly— he needs interactions with others."

"He can get that here, with your employees and with your other clients." Marin jerked her hand away. Her knuckles tingled from his gentle touch.

Philip sighed and opened his mouth, but before he could speak Marin rushed on.

"I looked carefully at the brochure, but I didn't see a fee. What is the charge for your service? Whatever it is, I'll double it if you'll allow me to bring John here during the day while I'm at work."

Philip scratched his chin, examining her from beneath lowered brows. "Doubled, huh? Well, that's pretty easy to figure, even for a mathematical wizard like me. Nothing times nothing is nothing."

Marin dropped her jaw. Had she heard correctly? "Nothing? You don't charge?"

Philip crossed his arms and grinned. "That's right. New Beginnings is non-profit. I don't charge my clients. The clients eventually are placed in a job situation where they draw a wage, so they stand to gain something; but I don't put a dollar amount on my service."

Marin's gaze swung around the building, taking in once more the tools and supplies and partitions and furnishings. "How do you keep this place going?"

"I receive a government stipend each month. The businesses that hire my clients pay a small percentage of the clients' salary to New Beginnings. But most of my resources come from private donations. People who believe in what I'm doing contribute." He frowned for a moment, worry creasing his brow, but then he seemed to deliberately relax the scowl lines and offered a small smile. "So you see—you can't bribe me."

"I'm not trying to bribe you." Marin used her sternest tone, although she was finding it increasingly difficult to be cross with this very likable, giving man. "I'm trying to persuade you. There's a difference."

Philip laughed, showing white even teeth. She liked the sound of his laugh and the crinkle lines on the outside of his brown eyes. He shook his head at her, still grinning. "A difference. Right, Marin. Look them up in a thesaurus—bet you'll find them side-by-side."

She ducked her head, trying not to smile at him. When she felt controlled, she raised her gaze and found him waiting, a sweet expression on his handsome face. Her heart caught in her throat. Swallowing, she started again. "Philip, I understand the purpose of your program. I admire it, and I can see you are sincere in what you want to do. But please understand where I am coming from. My parents wanted John protected. We all know too well how cruel the world can be. You're right that John is friendly. He'd talk to anyone. He'd *trust* anyone. And too many people aren't trustworthy." She took in a deep breath then blew it out. "If I were an employer hiring one of your clients, what would I probably pay an hour?"

Philip shrugged, seeming startled by her change in direction. "Average hourly wage is $6.50."

"How many hours a week does the average client put in?"

"Usually no more than thirty." Philip leaned back, giving her a speculative look. "Where are you heading with this?"

Marin held up her hand. "I'm an employer, willing to pay $10 an hour for forty hours a week. I want to hire my client to be one of your helpers. That comes to roughly $1,700 a month. That's what I'm offering you to allow John to become one of your employees at New Beginnings."

Philip's gaze narrowed. She didn't waver, just waited for him to decide. If this was a non-profit organization, no doubt he struggled as much as any other to keep the place afloat. She hoped her offer would be impossible for him to refuse.

It seemed as if hours passed before Philip finally straightened in his chair and opened his mouth to speak. "Marin, I want you to know I never intended New Beginnings to be a day-care facility. It goes against everything I believe in to keep your brother locked away from the world. God has a purpose for John, but if he's never allowed to experience anything beyond these four walls he may never find his purpose. To me, there's nothing sadder than a person who falls short of God's glorious plan for his life."

Marin felt her chest tighten. Philip's tone was gentle, but it hurt nonetheless.

"But right now I'm not seeing John as the real person in need. I see you as the one who is needy. So—*temporarily*—I'm willing to allow John to come here, just like any other employee, and be a custodian. But I'm emphasizing 'temporarily.' I want you to pray—pray hard!—about what is best for your brother. I'll allow him to remain here for one month." He held up one tapered finger to underscore his word. "At the end of John's month you're going to have to make a decision—either allow me to place John in a job outside of this warehouse, or you'll need to find another place for him to go."

five

Philip watched from the window as Marin and John Brooks made their way to the sporty car parked at the curb. He smiled as Marin handed John the keys and John aimed the keyless remote at the vehicle. John's pleasure in opening the locks was easily seen in the lift of his chin and the jaunty flip of his thumb on the button. Then he tossed Marin the keys. She caught them, threw her arm around John's shoulders in a quick hug, and brother and sister climbed in on opposite sides of the car. In moments they pulled away.

Marin was good with John, Philip acknowledged with a lift in his heart. He'd encountered many siblings whose own personal embarrassment at their brother or sister's limitations led them to be stilted or, worse, harsh. He admired Marin's ease in talking with John as if he mattered a great deal to her. Yet frustration built at her stubborn refusal to allow him to be with other people. Closing him off wasn't what was best—why couldn't she see that?

The memory surfaced, a wave of guilt rising with it. *God, I'm making up for that. Please take the memory away.* The prayer came automatically, a natural extension of the remembrance. Pushing himself off with his palm on the window frame, he headed back to the custodial corner. Anita would be starting at Burger King in three more days. They still had work to do.

❧

After only two weeks John was as settled in his new routine as if he had followed it for years. At supper he jabbered nonstop about "Philip this" and "Philip that," interjecting snippets about Eileen or Gregory or Andrew, some of the adult trainers who were employed by New Beginnings. Not once did John

49

balk about going but cheerfully put breakfast on the table each morning—bowls of corn flakes with chopped bananas—to help hurry Marin along. She wondered sometimes how he could have so quickly forgotten Mother and Dad and the old routine he'd shared with them.

This morning when she'd dropped him off, Marin had mentioned how easily he had adjusted, which was not typically in character for him. Philip had smiled and said, "Then it must be a God thing."

"A God thing," Marin now reflected aloud as she angled her car into her parking space at Brooks Advertising. She'd never heard the term before. In a way it almost sounded too casual to be appropriate for referring to the omnipotent Lord; yet it seemed natural coming from Philip. He firmly believed God had a hand in everything that came along life's pathway.

Well, she thought as she unlocked the front door and headed inside, *I hope Philip will see John's "employment" at New Beginnings as a "God thing" and keep him for more than a month. I haven't had time to make any other arrangements.*

Marin had slipped into her role as commander-in-chief of Brooks Advertising with a bit less ease than John had managed his change in routine. She sighed, the responsibility pressing like a knife between her shoulder blades. All of the employees were helpful and cooperative, but she felt she needed to stay two steps ahead to maintain her status as "boss." Being new to the role, it was more difficult than she could have imagined. How she wished she'd had an opportunity to ease into this position, but Dad's untimely death had changed everything.

But she didn't want to dwell on that again. Determinedly she pushed thoughts of Dad and Mother aside and focused on the here and now. She unlocked her private office, leaned her leather briefcase against the desk then sank down in Dad's executive chair and picked up the "to do" list waiting in the center of the large desk calendar. The list seemed a mile long. With a groan she dropped the paper and lowered her forehead to her hands.

"Marin?"

She popped upright, feeling a heat climb from her neck to her cheeks when she spotted Dick Ross hovering in the doorway. "Oh! Dick—I didn't hear you come in."

"I gathered that." He offered a smile and stepped completely into the office. His shoes echoed on the wooden floor. "You're here early."

Marin pushed her hair behind her ears and grimaced. "Yes. John was so eager to get to 'work' this morning that I couldn't slow him down. Something about its being donut day." She laughed lightly, shaking her head as she remembered him sitting in the car with his nose to the glass, watching for her to come out. He certainly enjoyed his time at New Beginnings.

"So that placement is working out well?" Dick's voice interrupted her reverie.

Marin lifted her gaze to meet Dick's. "Yes—yes, it's working out very well. But—" She broke off. She didn't need to share personal issues with Dick Ross. Why would he care that the placement would only last another couple of weeks? As she recalled, he had been one to encourage her to put John away somewhere. She had no desire to start that conversation again. Aunt Lenore was adversary enough on the issue!

Dick waited on the other side of the desk, his head tipped and brows angled high. She cleared her throat and crossed her arms, leaning back in the chair. "I'm sorry. Did you need something?"

"Yes, before the morning meeting, I wanted to go over. . ."

Dick pulled a chair up to Marin's desk and explained a problem he had with the amount of information Jefferson Landscaping wanted to include in a forty-five-second commercial. While they discussed how to present a compromise to the potential client, the front door opened and closed several times, signaling the arrival of the other employees.

At promptly eight thirty, Marin and Dick walked together to the conference room. By ten fifteen she was back in her office, determined to work her way through the first three items on her list before noon. At eleven thirty the telephone interrupted her concentration, and she spoke distractedly into the receiver. "Yes, Crystal?"

"Hi, Marin. I was wondering if you might be free for lunch today."

She gave a start. That wasn't the receptionist's voice on the other end. She pulled the receiver away from her ear, stared at it dumbly for a moment, then brought it back. "Who is this?"

A familiar chuckle rumbled through the line. "I'm sorry. I thought the receptionist introduced me. It's Philip Wilder."

At that moment Crystal appeared in the doorway, a frantic look on her face. She mouthed the words, "I'm sorry," and gestured broadly, obviously trying to explain something.

Marin shook her head at Crystal, scowling, unable to interpret the gestures.

"Marin? Are you there?" Philip's voice sounded in her ear.

"One minute, please," she told him then punched the mute button on the phone. "Crystal, what do you need?" She hoped her tone didn't sound as harried as she felt.

"I just wanted to apologize. I had two other calls when his"—she pointed at the telephone—"came through, and I accidentally sent it to you without checking with you first."

Marin waved her hand in dismissal. "Don't worry about it. It's fine." The front desk telephone rang shrilly, and she suggested, "Better go answer that." Crystal scuttled away. Marin dropped her head back, sighed, then released the mute to get back to Philip. "Hello? Are you still there?"

Another chuckle. Strange how that sound managed to soothe the edges of her frayed nerves. His voice followed. "Having a rough morning?"

"Not rough exactly, just busy," she clarified.

"So could you use a break?"

In the background a giggle erupted then was firmly shushed. The giggler was John. It followed that the shusher was Philip. She frowned. What was Philip up to? "What did you have in mind?" she asked cautiously.

"Well, John's done so well around here that he's earned a free lunch. He thought you might want to join us."

Of course John would want to include her. Of course it wasn't Philip's idea. For some reason disappointment niggled, but she firmly squashed it. She glanced at her wristwatch. "I suppose I could get away for a quick lunch. Where does John want to go?"

"He wants a Big Mac and French fries. Is that okay?"

The local McDonald's was only a few blocks from the office. That would mean less time away from work. "That's perfect," she said.

"Great! We'll see you at twelve?"

Another giggle could be heard, and Marin felt a pleased smile building. John was certainly comfortable with Philip. "I'll be there." She hung up, shaking her head. *A God thing.* It seemed Philip Wilder's friendship was a God thing, too. He and John were quite a pair.

❧

"Now remember, John," Philip repeated, leaning across the table to speak earnestly. "Let *me* bring up the job idea. If it's going to make Marin mad, I'd rather she was mad at me, okay?"

John wagged his head up and down. His almond-shaped eyes sparkled behind the wire rims of his glasses. "I will let her be mad at you. I will eat my ice cream and not say a word." He placed a thick finger against his own lips.

Philip winked his approval. John had done so well at the New Beginnings warehouse that all employees felt he should be given the opportunity to take a community position. Marin had made clear her feelings on the matter, but Philip was willing to go to bat for John. Working as a custodian in this very restaurant was one of Philip's clients—a man only two years older than John, also with Down's syndrome. If Marin saw Curtis successfully at work, surely it would help convince her John was just as capable.

Suddenly John exploded with giggles, pointing to the doors. "Here she is! Here she is!"

Philip leaned back to assume a casual pose, which was difficult with John chortling from across the table. He watched over his shoulder as Marin scanned the busy restaurant until she spotted them. He gave a quick wave, and she moved in their direction, the full skirt of her creamy two-piece dress swirling around her shapely ankles. He admired her appearance, which was always of professional elegance.

"Whew! It's crowded in here," she said by way of greeting. Sliding into the booth beside her brother, she nudged him with her shoulder. "What's so funny?"

John covered his mouth with both hands, which muffled his giggles, but his crinkling eyes proved the mirth was not controlled. Marin looked at Philip. "Have you two been telling jokes?"

John looked ready to explode, and other patrons were beginning to stare. To Marin, Philip explained, "I think he's just excited." Philip reached across the table and tapped John on the forearm. "Hey, buddy, no more giggling now, okay? You can't giggle and eat at the same time."

John dropped his hands to reveal pursed lips forming a huge, distorted grin.

Philip stifled an inward groan. John's theatrics, while somewhat humorous, were not timely considering the purpose of this meal out. How would he convince Marin that John was mature enough to handle a public employment situation if he couldn't get through a simple lunch without giggling like a child? Philip shrugged, sending Marin a weak smile. "Should we order?"

Marin raised her eyebrows, looking askance at her brother for a moment before answering. "Yes. Let's do."

They got in line behind three elderly women who smiled warmly in response to John's friendly hello. In the line next to them, however, was a young couple who openly stared at John as if he were a circus sideshow. Marin turned her back on the young couple, her jaw set, and Philip's heart turned over in his chest in sympathy. John appeared oblivious to the stares—he animatedly described what he planned to order, his stubby hands signing the words as he spoke—but Marin's discomfort was palpable.

John smiled broadly at the young cashier. The cashier kept her gaze angled toward the keyboard, which showed the menu options, while John cheerfully requested a Big Mac meal with super-sized fries and a soda. Marin leaned over and suggested he get the regular-sized order instead.

"But, Marin," he protested in a booming voice, "I like McDonald's French fries very much. I want lots of them."

The cashier, her chin still low, shifted her eyes to look curiously at John.

"There are lots of fries in a regular order, too, John. It's always been enough," Marin countered evenly.

"No, it is not enough. I want super-size today!" John thumped his fist on the counter.

The couple next to them snickered, and the cashier jumped slightly. All seemed focused on the interaction between John and Marin. Philip, listening, wondered if he should try to help Marin out, but he suspected she would resent his intrusion. Besides, he needed to see if John would allow this issue to be resolved. So he remained silent as Marin's cheeks flamed pink with embarrassment and John glared at her.

Marin glanced at her watching audience, offered them a weak smile of apology, then took a great breath, which seemed to calm her. Leaning toward John, she spoke in an even voice, barely above a whisper. "John, you may have super-sized fries *or* ice cream, but we can't do both. So you decide."

John rocked back and forth on his heels, a finger beneath

his chin, deep in thought. Finally he huffed and announced, "Regular fries. And a hot fudge sundae." His voice carried over all the other restaurant noise.

Marin made another quick glance around before nodding to her brother. "Good choice." She quickly gave her order then stepped back to allow Philip to move forward. His chest swelled with pity. John had settled down, but people still watched, as if expecting an encore. Marin's hazel eyes looked unnaturally bright, and he feared she might break down and cry. As he reached for his wallet to pay for their food, he suggested she and John go sit down while he waited for their order.

By the time Philip returned to the table, tray in hand, Marin and John had apparently made their peace. They were visiting quietly, and no sign of John's earlier tantrum was seen in either face. The moment the tray touched the table, John reached eagerly for the wrapped food items.

"I will hand things out," he said, beaming. "I remember what you ordered." With great ceremony he placed Marin's chicken sandwich and iced tea in front of her then gave Philip his burger, fries, and soft drink. His tongue poked out as he took his own items and popped the lid off the sundae. Stretching his hands toward Marin and Philip, he said, "Pray."

Philip took John's hand then reached for Marin's. She flushed slightly but placed her hand in his. He gave it a quick squeeze before bowing his head and offering a simple blessing for the meal. At the "amen" John pulled away immediately, but Marin wrapped her fingers around Philip's hand and held tight for a moment. He tightened his own grip, offering his understanding, and at last she pulled away.

John gobbled his food, and Marin leaned over to whisper in his ear. He slowed his pace. Marin smirked and snitched one of his fries. He grinned as she dipped it in ketchup and raised it to her lips. After she swallowed, she turned to Philip. "What did John do to earn this meal out?"

She had given him a perfect lead in. Philip took a sip of his drink before answering. "The clients earn points by following directions, finishing tasks within a specified time limit, staying on task—those types of things. If you're going to have a job, you've got to be able to stay focused from beginning to end, right?" He pointed at her with a French fry. "John earned as many points in two weeks as many of our clients earn in a whole month. He's done a great job."

Marin smiled at John. "That's terrific! I'm proud of you."

John lifted a spoonful of drippy sundae and slurped it. Speaking around the biteful, he said, "But I cannot tell you what will happen now. You will get mad. Right, Philip?"

Philip sucked in a breath as Marin's gaze spun in his direction. He watched her brows come down—in curiosity or irritation? Tipping her head, she fixed Philip with a stern look that made him wish he were someplace else.

"What exactly has John been instructed not to share with me?"

Lord, Philip prayed inwardly, *help me choose my words here.* He pushed aside his burger and rested his elbows on the edge of the table. "Well, Marin, I hoped to talk to you about—"

At that moment Philip felt a hearty clap against his shoulder. Marin's gaze shifted sharply, and Philip turned his head to find a familiar face smiling down at him.

"Hi, Philip!"

Philip forced a smile, his gaze skittering between Marin and the newcomer. He swallowed. "Hi, Curtis."

From the look on Marin's face no further explanation would be needed. She knew.

six

Marin wadded up the paper wrapper from her sandwich and dropped it on the empty tray. She wanted to throw it—hard—at Philip, but ever mindful that she was setting an example for John, she kept a rein on her temper.

A setup. This whole lunch had been a setup. Nothing more than a way for her to see one of Philip's clients in action so she would bow to Philip's discretion in placing John in such a job. Well, it wasn't going to work. She was not so easily manipulated, and Philip Wilder better learn that right now!

Ignoring Philip's contrite look, she gave John a quick peck on the cheek, grabbed her purse, and rose to her feet in one fluid motion. Smoothing her skirt, she said stiffly, "Thank you very much for the lunch, Mr. Wilder." Turning to John, she added with a bit more warmth, "I'll see you around five, John." And she spun on the heel of her off-white pump and marched out of the restaurant without a backward glance.

Fury filled her chest, increasing with every staccato step that led her back to the office. She had walked—it wasn't far, and it was such a pretty day. Now she was grateful for the opportunity to dispel some of this frustration before she returned to the office.

Who did he think he was, filling John's head with notions of jobs and working? Hadn't she made it perfectly clear that John in a workplace was a subject not open for discussion? She paid dearly to have John in the protected environment of New Beginnings, and as long as Philip took her check each week he would follow her rules!

She stopped at an intersection and squinted against the sun, impatiently waiting for the red light to change to green so she could continue her stomping progress. Though her feet stilled, her thoughts raged on. Philip hadn't been around John long enough to make a determination about his readiness for a job. Of course John did well at the warehouse—all success elements were in place: few people around, a secure setting, lots of attention. Most of the time John did well at home, too, but even there he had his moments.

The light changed, and Marin stepped off the curb, her face hot as she remembered the embarrassment of John's brief tantrum in McDonald's. At home, with no audience, she felt equipped to handle John's erratic moments even if she'd prefer not to. In public it was a completely different ballgame.

She relived the snickering and curious glances. A knot formed in her stomach. Philip had surely been aware of how John's behavior had captured everyone's attention—the sympathetic pressure on her hand as he'd prayed made clear he felt compassion for what she had experienced. But what Philip didn't realize was that John could stir that kind of reaction simply by walking into a room—he didn't have to throw a tantrum for people to snicker and stare.

And that was why John didn't belong in public places. Not on his own. Not without Marin to act as a buffer. Sadness battled with the anger, seeking equal footing. Her steps slowed. Philip had obviously wanted her to see his client— what was his name? Curtis?—in action. Well, instead Philip got to see John in action. Now maybe he would understand why it wasn't possible for John to take a job in public. John was. . .unpredictable. And people were. . .morbidly curious. She would not allow him to be gawked at like an animal displayed in a zoo cage. Today the reaction didn't go beyond a few rude sniggers and open stares. But she knew real cruelty could sometimes follow.

Marin reached Brooks Advertising and paused outside the doors, taking big breaths to calm her unsteady nerves. *Philip Wilder will have to be made to understand that John is not to be taken to public places without my permission,* she determined. *And I better start hunting right now for someplace else for him to go.*

She felt a prick of guilt—John enjoyed New Beginnings so much. It would be hard for him to leave. But, she reminded herself as she stepped into the cool reception area and headed for her office, if he adjusted to this change he could adjust to another. He would have to.

❧

Philip slapped the ledger closed with more force than was necessary. Across the room the lone remaining employee, Eileen, raised her gaze from rinsing the sink and queried, "Problem?"

Philip sighed. "Eileen, would you come over here? Maybe you can help me with something." He had tried to keep his financial woes secret from his employees—no need to scare them into seeking other employment—but Eileen had been with him from the planning stages of New Beginnings. He knew he could trust her to keep a tight lip but also be a support.

She snatched up a cotton towel and carried it with her, drying her hands as she crossed the floor. Early sixties, chunky but solid, with tight gray curls, compliments of a home wave, Eileen looked like anybody's grandma. Philip smiled as she settled her bulk in the plastic chair next to him and flopped the damp towel on the corner of his desk.

"You looking all long-faced there because of Marin Brooks?"

Her question caught Philip off guard. He raised his brows. "Huh?"

Eileen smirked and pointed at him. "You haven't fooled any of us. We've been watching you." She linked her fingers and rested her hands on her belly. "You're a personable man, Philip, and you're friendly to everyone. But it's different with this Marin Brooks."

Philip felt his heart begin to clamor. Cautiously he questioned, "How so?"

Eileen shrugged. "Little things. The smile in your eyes when she drops off or picks up her brother. The quicker step you use when she's at the door, like you're hoping to gain a little more time with her. The extra few minutes you spend just chatting with John." She laughed, picking up the towel and flapping it against his arm. "Stop looking so stricken. Being interested in a pretty girl isn't the end of the world. You're a young man—a handsome one at that. I'd say it was high time you expressed that kind of interest."

"But you don't understand," Philip protested. Eileen and the others weren't aware of his arrangement with Marin. His additional interest in her was due to the short amount of time he had to convince her to allow John to remain in his program. Wasn't it?

Eileen interrupted his thoughts. "She seemed upset tonight. Something happen?"

Philip replayed Marin's cool reception to his attempt at conversation when she retrieved John this afternoon. Upset was an understatement. She had appeared to simmer with controlled fury. He feared he had messed up things permanently. But she hadn't said she wouldn't bring John back, so perhaps there was still hope.

"Philip?"

Philip realized Eileen was waiting for an answer. He sighed again and leaned back in his chair. "We had a little. . . setback. . .when I took John for lunch. Marin came, too—at John's request." Eileen smirked at that, but Philip ignored her and went on. "John wanted a super-sized meal, and Marin suggested he stick to regular-sized. John got a little upset." He realized he was downplaying the outburst, but Eileen had worked with people with disabilities long enough to understand the picture without his outlining every detail. "Stirred things up for a bit, but he settled down pretty quickly. Marin was embarrassed, though, and I think she's irritated that I took him out."

Eileen frowned. "Seems odd she'd be angry at you if it was John who created the uproar."

Philip dropped his gaze, running his thumb over the edge of the desk. "Well, she's mad because I kind of pulled a sneaky trick."

"You?" Eileen draped the towel across her knees and leaned forward, her eyes bright with interest. "A sneaky trick?" Her tone indicated she didn't believe Philip capable of underhandedness.

Philip nodded, sheepishly meeting her gaze. "Yeah. See, Marin is really opposed to John taking a position in the public eye."

"Then what is he—?"

Philip held up his hand, interrupting her flow of words. "She's worried about how people will treat him. But you know Curtis is doing real well at McDonald's, so I thought if she saw Curtis at work she'd realize John could be just as successful." Shaking his head, he finished ruefully, "But John threw a hissy fit, and half the restaurant stared as if they'd never seen anything like it before. Then Curtis came to the table before I had a chance to say anything to her, and I could tell by the look on her face she knew she'd been had. I really blew it."

Eileen clucked. "Oh, now, Philip. She'll get over it. She was probably still feeling uncomfortable about the way people reacted to John's outburst. I know from experience how that can discombobulate your sense of self-esteem. But you'll see. When she comes in tomorrow she'll be her same sweet self. So stop fretting."

Philip released a brief huff of laughter. "To be honest, Eileen, I'm not fretting over Marin. Somehow I'll work that problem out. It's. . ." He scratched his head, wondering if it was fair to dump this on Eileen. She loved working here— with her husband dead and all her children grown and moved away, the New Beginnings clients were a surrogate family to her. How would she react to the possibility of losing it all? Yet he needed a sounding board.

"Go ahead, Philip. Spill it."

Eileen's brisk, no-nonsense tone was the deciding factor. He flipped the ledger open and pointed to the last numbers in each of the columns. Eileen leaned forward, reading along the lines, and her graying brows formed a sharp V. She pointed to each number with a work-roughened finger, her lips pursed in obvious concentration. At last she looked up, disbelief coloring her expression. "Are these numbers accurate?"

Philip nodded. "I'm afraid so." He closed the ledger again, an attempt to shut away the problem. "My biggest contributor stopped contributing. No explanation given, but the account was closed." He tapped the cover of the ledger book. "There might be enough funds for full operation for one more month—maybe six weeks if I batten down the hatches and don't take any new clients. But beyond that. . . ?"

"Oh, Philip. . ." Eileen's sympathetic tone touched Philip's heart. They sat for a few minutes in silence, digesting this information. Then suddenly Eileen straightened in her chair and slapped her palms to her thighs. "Well, then, we've got work to do, don't we? We need to brainstorm. Come up with some ways to bring in more funds." She grasped Philip's hand and shook it. "But first we need to pray. Close your eyes."

Philip closed his eyes and listened as Eileen petitioned the Lord in a clear, sure voice. Emotion pressed at his chest as he silently echoed every word of her request. Part of a verse from John's Gospel flittered through his memory: *"Ask and you will receive. . . ."* In the quiet building, with Eileen's warm palm pressed to his, her confident voice raised in communication, he felt the Lord's presence.

She finished, "Thank You for working this out to Your glory. Amen." Giving his hand another firm pat, she said, "Now no more fretting. Look again at the verse you have painted on the banner and remember that the Lord prepared you for this work. He won't let you down."

Philip offered a smile, his gaze moving to the words boldly displayed over the work area. He did believe in Ephesians 2:10—every person was created to perform good works, and he knew without a doubt God had placed this work on his heart. Eileen was right—somehow his financial problems would be solved. "Thanks, Eileen. You're a good friend."

Eileen snorted, but she smiled at him. "Yes, well, right now my cat is probably wondering why his good friend hasn't come home to feed him. So I better *git*." She stood and headed toward the door at a brisk pace. Before she left, however, she looked back over her shoulder and added, "I'll be praying that Marin gets over her mad, too, because I don't figure you'll be able to concentrate on much of anything else until you're on the rights with her again."

"Go home, Eileen," Philip ordered dryly. His cheeks twitched with the effort of controlling his smile.

She hooted with laughter and stepped out the door, sealing the warehouse in silence.

Philip propped his heels on the desk next to the ledger and allowed his gaze to return to the painted words displayed over his head. He read aloud, " 'For we are God's workmanship, created in Christ Jesus to do good works, which God prepared in advance for us to do.' " He scowled for a moment, recalling that despite God's preparations, many did not choose to do good works. Rocky immediately came to mind, and his heart clenched as he wondered what his brother might be doing these days.

But he really didn't want to think about Rocky. Keeping New Beginnings going was top priority, and that's where he would keep his focus. Thumping his feet to the floor, he announced, "New Beginnings was formed to do good works, and somehow it will continue to do good works." *Maybe saying it out loud will help it be true.* He scooped up the ledger, opened his top drawer, and dropped the book inside. Shutting the drawer firmly, he rose and went through the lockup routine by rote. With the building secure he straddled his motorcycle and turned his thoughts toward home.

But suddenly, as if by their own accord, his thoughts changed course. A second problem required immediate attention. Marin and John. Somehow he had to find a permanent placement for John before his self-imposed time limit. He had no time to waste.

He made a snap decision. Instead of going to his own home, he'd go see Marin and John. They didn't live far from the city park where he had spent summer hours during his growing-up years. The Bible admonished believers not to go to bed angry, so he'd just help Marin not break that biblical demand. With a twist of his wrist the cycle engine throttled to a steady hum. He aimed the bike in the direction of Park Street.

seven

Marin sat on the front porch, the cordless phone pressed to her ear. The early evening breeze felt pleasant against her bare legs, and she stretched them out to catch the last of the waning sun. Behind her, through the open screen door, she could hear John thumping around in the kitchen, organizing the recyclables, as Michael W. Smith crooned from the radio. Across the street a half dozen grade-school age boys kicked a soccer ball back and forth across the yard, cheering each other on. Sometimes she had to strain to hear the soft voice of Aunt Chris, but she refused to give up her pleasant perch.

Marin answered her aunt's question. "Yes, John loves going there. That isn't the issue. The issue is that it isn't a day-care facility, and the owner has made it clear he won't allow John to stay there longer than a month."

"Are you sure he wouldn't reconsider since it's working out well for John?"

Marin scowled, remembering Philip's ploy at noon. Her tone turned hard. "I doubt it. He's already making noises about it, and John's only been there two weeks."

"Well," came Chris's reasonable voice, "maybe you should consider what he suggests."

Marin nearly swallowed the telephone. "Consider it? Aunt Chris! You know how protective Mother always was with John! Why, she'd turn over in her grave if I even thought about letting him take some sort of job."

A goal was made in the soccer game, and the boys jumped in a circle, screeching in joy. Marin pressed the phone tighter to her ear to hear. All she caught was, ". . .was necessarily best for John."

"I'm sorry—what did you say?"

She was thankful the noisy throng across the street dropped to the grass to rest, so she was able to hear clearly.

"I said, although I know Mary did what she thought was in John's best interests, Darin didn't always agree it was necessarily best for John."

Marin felt stunned by this. Her father had never indicated he wanted anything different done with John. At least he'd never voiced it to her. "How do you know that?" she asked as she toyed with the frayed edge of her denim cut-offs.

Marin could almost hear the smile in Chris's tone as she answered. "Marin, darling, your father and I were very close. He shared a great deal with me—his pride in you, his worry for John, his love for Mary. He understood your mother's fears, and he also understood she and John had a tighter bond than the one that existed between him and his son. So he allowed Mary to make the decisions where John was concerned."

Reeling, Marin pressed, "So do you think Dad wanted John put in some—some institution?"

"Absolutely not!" Aunt Chris's adamant tone carried through the line. "Never an institution. John is too high functioning to require that type of placement, although it's perfectly acceptable and even desirable for some families. But I know at one time he did look into some group homes. Your mother was very much opposed, though, so he dropped the idea."

"But Dad always told me I'd be responsible for John when he and Mom were gone."

"Marin, you do realize being responsible doesn't have to mean giving up your whole life for him, don't you?"

No, Marin hadn't realized that. She'd always envisioned herself assuming her mother's role, maintaining the home, caring for John. She didn't know how to respond.

Aunt Chris spoke again. "Listen, honey, whatever you decide, I know you'll pray about it, and you'll make an unselfish decision with John's best interests at heart. I have confidence in you, just as your dad did. And whenever you need to talk, you remember I'm just a phone call away."

Tears pricked behind Marin's lids. How she appreciated her aunt's support. If only Aunt Lenore, who lived blocks away rather than states away, could be so helpful. She uttered a brief, silent prayer for Aunt Lenore to somehow become more like Aunt Chris. "Thanks, Aunt Chris. Oh, by the way—"

A distant growl intruded, and Marin lifted her head, seeking the source of the noise. The boys across the street also turned as a group, and their faces lit with delight as a bright blue and chrome motorcycle turned the corner and roared onto their street. To Marin's surprise the cycle slowed in front of her house and pulled directly into the driveway. The rider killed the motor then reached up to remove his helmet. Marin felt her heart skip a beat when she recognized the rumpled brown hair of Philip Wilder emerging from beneath the shimmering helmet.

"By the way, what?" came Chris's voice.

"Aunt Chris, I've got company. Can I call you later?" They said their good-byes, and Marin placed the phone on the porch, rising as Philip swung his leg over the bike.

"Hey, mister," one of the boys called from across the street, "that's a neat motorcycle! Can we come see it?"

Philip grinned and waved his large hand. "Sure, come on over."

With a rush the boys raced across the street to surround Philip and the cycle.

Marin stood on the porch watching him interact with the boys, listening to him answer their boisterous questions, wondering why he was here. The screen door opened, and John emerged. When he spotted Philip, he broke into a huge smile.

"Philip!" John ambled down the porch steps in his awkward gait. "You came over!"

The boys saw John, and their withdrawal was immediate. It nearly broke Marin's heart to see how their expressions became wary, uncertain. John was harmless—why couldn't these children see it?

The one who had asked permission to come over gestured to his buddies. "Well, thanks, mister, but we gotta go. Come on, guys." Marin heard one of them mutter, "Didn't know a retarded guy lived over there." The group headed back to their own yard and disappeared behind the house. The parting words stabbed like a knife in Marin's chest.

If John heard the comment, he was too excited to care. He pounded Philip's back and jabbered, unconcerned. "Philip, I like this motorcycle! It is very blue and shiny. Is it yours?"

Philip draped his arm around John's shoulders. "Yep, it sure is, buddy. Maybe someday I can take you for a ride."

"Today?" John leaned toward Philip eagerly. "We can go for a ride today?"

Philip shook his head. "Not today, John. I didn't bring my extra helmet, and you should always wear a helmet when you ride a motorcycle. But if it's all right with Marin I'll bring the bike back, and we'll go for a ride one evening soon, okay?"

John hurried to where Marin remained perched on the top step, her bare toes curled over the concrete edge. "Marin, will that be okay? Will it be okay for Philip to take me for a ride? When he has his extra helmet?"

Marin smiled. "Sure, John. Philip and I will work it out." She came down one step, putting herself on an equal level with John. "Did you get the recycling finished?"

He shook his head. "There is more."

"Well, the truck comes tomorrow," she reminded him. "Better finish up."

John looked forlornly toward Philip and the cycle. "But Philip is here."

Philip now stepped forward. "I'll be here for a while, John. Go ahead and finish up. I'll wait till you're done, then we can visit before I leave."

Satisfied, John padded into the house. Philip crossed the sidewalk to stand at the bottom of the porch and look up at Marin. He squinted as the rosy sun slanted across his face. "I hope it's okay that I just dropped by. I wanted to talk to you."

Aunt Chris's revelations still in her ears, Marin wasn't sure she was emotionally prepared to listen to anything Philip had to say. She grasped the porch railing for support. "What about?"

"Lunch. And why I invited you."

Marin shifted her gaze. His brown eyes were too sincere, too penetrating. He had a very unsettling effect on her emotions. "I think it was fairly clear. And there really isn't anything to discuss."

"I think there is."

She slowly brought her gaze back around. He waited patiently, a slight smile tipping up the corners of his lips. He held his helmet against his hip, causing his light jacket to hang open. His green T-shirt fit snugly against his chest, which appeared defined, as if he lifted weights. Although he stood two steps below her, his height put him almost even with her. Altogether he created a pleasing package. She was suddenly acutely aware of her ratty jean shorts, stretched-out T-shirt, and bare feet. What must he think of her scruffy appearance? Her tummy trembled slightly as she realized it mattered what Philip thought of her.

He lifted one booted foot and placed it next to her toes. In a near whisper he asked, "Will you at least allow me to apologize?"

Marin suddenly discovered she was holding her breath. She released it in a whoosh then waved her hands in dismissal. "You don't need to apologize. It was just a—a mess with so many people crowding around and John getting upset, and I'd already had a very busy morning, which made me rather short-tempered, so—" She broke off as he burst into laughter.

Well! She was trying to set things right, and all he could do was laugh about it. "What's so funny?" she demanded.

He swallowed, obviously trying to gain control. "I'm sorry. I wasn't really laughing at you, but when you said you were short-tempered. . ." He smirked. "Really, Marin, if that was your best shot at being short-tempered, I'd say I have nothing to worry about."

Despite herself she had to smile. She had been so irritated with him, had felt almost betrayed by his blatant attempt to change her mind; but standing here in the splashes of sunlight that brought out the golden highlights in his tousled hair, she found the anger dissolved. All that remained was a slight discomfort. And right now she couldn't completely identify the source of that discomfort.

Philip smiled again, lifting his shoulder. "Come on, Marin. Let's sit down here and let me try to explain something to you." As if certain of her acquiescence, he turned and seated himself on the third step. He rested his helmet on his left knee and cupped one broad hand over it to hold it there. Looking up at her, he added, "Please?"

She sighed. Philip Wilder was a difficult man to resist. She scooted to the opposite end of the steps and perched sideways, her back against the wrought iron railing. She pulled her bare heels close to her hips and wrapped both arms around her legs. The position gave her a measure of security. "I'm listening."

"Good." Shadows from the oak tree in the yard veiled his features as he began to speak softly. "First of all, I want you to know I understand and respect your feelings about keeping John safe. I've worked with people with handicaps long enough to know the world isn't always a welcoming place for those who are different."

Marin nodded. "Like those boys just now," she blurted out. The hurt was still fresh. "You saw how they all disappeared when John came out. He's no monster." She heard the defensiveness in her tone, but she couldn't seem to hold it in.

"Of course, he's not," Philip agreed. "He's John—gentle John. We know that because we know him. And if those boys took the time to know him, they'd find it out, too. But chances are they will never get to know John. Partly because of their own misconceptions about disabilities, and partly because. . .you won't allow it."

Marin tightened the hold on her knees. "That isn't fair, Philip. You don't know what my family has been through with John. Believe me when I say we have our reasons for keeping him away from people like those boys."

"I don't doubt that," Philip countered. "I'm sure you've been hurt over and over again by people's misconceptions."

"It's not just misconceptions!" Marin burst out, the hurtful comment made by the boy leaving her yard replaying itself in her memory. "It's out-and-out meanness! And it hurts so much when people—" She broke off, abashed, as tears formed and spilled down her cheeks. She dashed them away with shaking fingertips, but not before Philip had seen them.

His brown eyes softened with understanding concern. "I'm so sorry you've been hurt, Marin. I wish I could change what's happened. I can't do that—I can't rewrite the past." His face clouded for a moment, his forehead crinkling as if struck by a sharp pain. Then the expression cleared, and he added, "But I believe we can make the future better, if we work together."

Marin affected a harsh tone to control her sadness. "How?"

"By changing people's perceptions."

Again she barked one word. "How?"

Philip leaned toward her, his deep voice assuming a whisper-softness. "Think about it, Marin. It's only our perception of being retarded that makes it a negative thing. Consider music—the retards in music give a different feel. The music becomes restful, relaxing, welcoming. People have taken the word *retarded* and turned it into something bad. But really, retarded simply means slowed down. Being relaxed, rested.

Most retarded people are so loving and welcoming—they just reach out to you. How can that be a bad thing? In itself it isn't. It's our reaction to it that makes it negative.

"So there's my goal—to educate others on what it means to be retarded. To help them look below the surface to the soul of the person. Maybe I can build an understanding empathy, and people will become more accepting of their developmentally delayed peers. It can happen, Marin. I believe it."

"But how, Philip? How can it happen?" When she asked this time, it wasn't with anger or defensiveness but with a real desire to know the answer.

"It can happen when people like John spend time with people like you and me, and they discover just how much alike they are."

Marin shook her head. "It sounds wonderful, Philip, but it isn't realistic. How can I expect 'the world' to accept John when people in my own family—people who've known him his whole life—can't accept him?"

Philip leaned against the railing and looked at her with his eyelids lowered. She felt as if he were trying to peer below the surface of her skin and see what was underneath. After a long time of silence, while crickets took up their night chorus and the sun slipped behind rooftops, he finally spoke. "You're scared. I see that. I even understand it—more than you know, I understand it. But someday, Marin, you're going to have to release that fear and let John go. Because a life shut away accomplishes nothing, and I can't accept for even one minute that 'nothing' is what God has in mind for your brother."

Before Marin could respond, the screen door swung open, and John stepped onto the porch. "All the recycling is done," he announced. "Now I can visit." His hands chopped out the sign for *visit* as he plunked himself in the wedge of space between Philip and Marin.

Marin quickly rose. "Yes, you two visit. I'll be inside." She stepped into the house before Philip could say anything else.

She walked through the dark hallway to Dad's office, turned on his desk light, and sat in his chair. Propping her chin in her hands, she stared at the family picture on the corner of the desk. How she wished her parents were here in person rather than merely captured on photo paper.

"Dad," she whispered, "did you really want something more for John?" Tipping her head, she examined her father's warm smile. "Why didn't you ever talk to me about John? What else didn't I know about you, Daddy?"

Marin had always gravitated toward her father. She knew this was partly because Mother was always so involved with John and partly because she and Dad shared so many common interests. But now, to her great regret, she realized she and her father had never discussed the most important things. "Maybe you thought we'd have time. . .later," she said to the portrait.

She reflected on the day of her college graduation. Mom and Dad had left John with Dick Ross's family, so for the first time she'd had their full, undivided attention for an entire weekend. She'd relished those moments, basked in their pride, anticipated the evolving relationship that included friendship. When they'd gone to supper after the graduation ceremony, Dad had toasted her with iced tea and announced, "To Marin, the future of Brooks Advertising!" Then he'd lowered the glass, smiled at her indulgently, and added softly, "Ah, Marin, what plans I have for you. . . ."

They had fully intended to discuss those plans when Marin returned home the following week, but the opportunity was lost. Only a few hours later—Mother was eager to return home, to John—Dad pulled in front of a semi, and their lives were finished. And Marin's life—the life she had planned for herself—was finished, too.

Resentment pressed upward.

Regret mingled with it.

A hoot of laughter carried from the porch to the office.

Resolve pushed the other emotions away. For whatever reason, God had chosen to take her parents home, and John was now her responsibility. She would never know for sure what her father had planned for his son, but she had no doubt in her mind what her mother wanted. For now, she would continue what her mother began.

The motorcycle rumbled to life, and she crossed to the window, peeking between the wooden slats of the blinds to see Philip on the bike. Dark strands of hair curled around the bottom edge of the bright blue helmet, and Marin thought, *He needs a haircut.* John hovered close by, nearly dancing in excitement. In the yard across the street, two boys stood, obviously imitating John. Marin clenched her jaw.

Philip's head turned toward the house, no doubt seeking her, but she remained unmoving even while her heart tugged at her to go and say good-bye. As soon as he pulled away she went to the door and called, "John, come on in now."

John ambled up the driveway, humming an aimless, off-tune melody. As he entered the house, he gave her an impulsive hug. "I love you, Marin."

Marin felt the sting of tears. "I love you, too, John." She did. She really did.

Humming again, John released her and headed toward his bedroom. He shut the door, leaving Marin alone. She stayed in the doorway, considering marching across the street and taking those boys to task for their rude behavior. But then she heaved a sigh. What good would it do? She closed the door and turned to the empty room.

More than any other time since her parents' death, Marin wished she had somebody else in this house to talk to. Someone with whom she could share these tumbling emotions. Someone who would just listen and not tell her what to think or feel. Philip's face appeared in her memory— his open, handsome, friendly face. But she pushed the thought aside. He would certainly do more than listen—he would tell her what he thought she should do, and she didn't want to hear it.

Dropping onto the couch, she brought up her knees and wrapped her arms around them. She closed her eyes and whispered, "Oh, Mom and Dad, I miss you so much."

eight

Rays of early morning sunlight crept between the slats of the blinds and inched their way across Marin's rumpled comforter. She lay, propped on pillows, and watched the golden bands creep ever closer until a shaft of light assaulted her eyes. With a groan she pulled the sheet over her head and wiggled a little lower on the mattress, knowing if the sun's rays had disturbed her slumber they had no doubt disturbed John's. And he would expect company when he awakened.

Sure enough, as if her thoughts could make it happen, a light tap sounded on her bedroom door. She sighed. "Come on in, John."

The door swung wide, and John appeared, his sleepy eyes wide with confusion. "How did you know it was me, Marin?"

She stifled a laugh. "Well, who else is here?"

He blinked twice, digesting this. "Only me," he finally said. He stepped closer to the bed. "It is Sunday."

She yawned. "I know."

"It is pancakes day."

Marin nodded. She knew. "Give me another minute or two, would you please?"

He turned complacently but paused in the doorway. "One minute or two minutes?"

Marin shook her head. John would stand in front of the kitchen clock and count down the seconds, reappearing in either one or two minutes, whichever she decided. She threw back the covers. "I'm getting up."

He grinned. "I will be in the kitchen!"

❧

Philip tossed back the sheet and bounced out of bed, reaching

77

into an all-over stretch the moment his feet hit the floor. Shivering—he'd left the window open last night—he crossed to the sliding glass doors that led to a small concrete patio outside his bedroom and peeked out at the new day. The yard, which fell west of the apartment complex, still lay in full shadow, but he spotted two robins pecking for worms in the sparse grass. He scratched his chin, reminding himself that he hadn't gotten around to dumping that fertilizer he'd bought to help thicken the grass cover.

Well, he wouldn't be doing it today. Today was the Lord's Day.

And this Lord's Day was his first day of teaching Sunday school. A smile tugged at his cheeks as he considered the prospect. He'd been a Sunday school attendee for years, but teaching? Not something he figured he'd do. When Reverend Lowe had asked him, though, he hadn't been able to say no. It meant a change in routine—normally he slept in on Sundays then attended Sunday school and the late church service, but now that he was a teacher he felt the need to attend the early service and be fed before he tried to feed his own little flock.

Rubbing his hands together in anticipation, he chose his clothing, including a tie, which sported sheep grazing on a grassy pasture—*to remind me of my little flock*—then hopped into the shower. While he stood beneath the jets of steaming water, he reviewed the lesson he had planned for the junior high boys. He hoped the boys would be as enthusiastic about learning as he felt about teaching. He smiled, remembering the teacher who had led him to the Lord when he was a troubled eighth grader. He owed a huge debt of gratitude to Mr. Spence, and he hoped to repay it by being as good an influence on his students as Mr. Spence had been on him.

Only forty minutes after rising to greet the day, Philip was behind the wheel of his battered pickup truck, heading to Central Community Church. He pulled to the farthest corner of the parking lot. Only a handful of cars decorated the expansive parking area, and Philip chuckled to himself. *Guess I was more excited than I thought—I beat nearly everyone here.* He gave a shrug, whistling, as he strode across the asphalt and up the sidewalk leading to the worship sanctuary. *But it'll be great for me to hear the early sermon before I teach the boys.*

He shook hands with the greeter, accepted a bulletin, then found an aisle seat in one of the first few rows of pews, his heart already looking ahead to what Reverend Lowe had prepared to share.

"Marin, why on earth do you let him sit there by himself?"

Aunt Lenore whispered in deference to their surroundings, but her strident voice carried beyond Marin's ears. The row of teenagers in front of them turned to peek over their shoulders. She raised her eyebrows at them, and they turned back around.

John loved sitting in the pew directly in front of the sound booth. It rested at the foot of the center aisle of church and gave him a straight view to the pulpit and choir loft. He claimed it was the best seat in the house, and Mother had always allowed him to sit there. Marin saw no reason why she should change the arrangement just because Aunt Lenore didn't approve. Aunt Lenore approved of nothing where John was concerned.

Leaning close to Lenore's ear, she explained quietly, "He enjoys sitting where he can see everything. He and Mother called it his 'special pew.' The sound booth technicians don't mind—it doesn't hurt anything."

Aunt Lenore shook her head, clicking her tongue against her teeth. "I think it's asking for trouble, leaving him completely unattended."

Frustration welled. Aunt Lenore was Mother's twin, but Lenore had none of Mother's gentleness and compassion. Marin wanted to poke her aunt hard in the ribs and tell her to mind her own business, but church was not a place for confrontation. Instead she forced herself to whisper calmly. "He's fine. Trust me."

Marin sent a glance in John's direction. He sat quietly, a bulletin in his stubby hands, his ankles crossed. When he spotted Marin looking at him, he gave a little wave. Marin smiled and waved back with two fingers.

She turned her focus to the pulpit where Reverend Lowe began his sermon. Only five minutes into the delivery, a mild commotion broke out behind her. Assuming a small child was wrestling with his or her parent, she kept her eyes facing forward, but Lenore turned around. She emitted a gasp and clamped her hand painfully on Marin's knee.

"Marin, do something!" Lenore hissed.

Marin looked over her shoulder to see John standing in front of his pew, waving his hand and beaming broadly. "Hello! Hello!" His raspy voice, while a whisper, carried clearly.

"Make him sit down!" Lenore ordered through clenched teeth. Her neck and cheeks were mottled with anger.

Marin, her face hot with embarrassment, gestured to John. He looked at her, but instead of settling down he became more animated. Now that he had Marin's attention, he pointed with both hands and laughed out loud.

Lenore nearly pushed Marin out of the pew. "Get him out of here before he ruins the entire service!"

Marin stumbled into the aisle, regained her footing, and went to John as quickly as her high-heeled sandals would allow. Though she kept her gaze straight ahead, she could feel the curious looks following her progress, and she was certain her face was as red as the dress she wore.

"Marin, it is Philip," John said when she reached him.

Without responding, she looped her arm through his and directed him toward a set of double doors leading to the foyer.

"It is Philip right over there," John continued, too excited to remember that talking aloud in church was against the rules.

Once they were in the foyer, well away from the doors,

Marin wheeled on her brother. "John, what got into you? You know better than to create a scene in church! Mother and Dad would be so disappointed in you!"

John's smile faded, and his shoulders drooped. "But—but I saw Philip."

"You couldn't have seen Philip. Philip doesn't attend our church," Marin argued, her embarrassment displaying itself in anger. "But even if you had, you know better than to stand up and wave and talk. You won't be able to sit in the special pew anymore if you can't stay quiet."

Tears glittered in John's eyes. "I am sorry."

His genuine remorse completely dissolved Marin's anger, but it couldn't remove her humiliation. "I know you are, John, but Aunt Lenore is really mad. You can't stand up and talk in church."

John nodded, his expression sad. "But I only said hi to Philip."

Marin blew out a breath. "That's not the point, John. You can't talk *at all*."

At that moment the doors from the sanctuary opened again. Marin cringed, anticipating Aunt Lenore's thundering presence, but her jaw dropped when she saw who it was.

A huge grin split John's face, and he held out his arms. "Philip!"

Philip whispered, "Hi, John." He strode across the carpet to join them.

John opened his arms for a hug, which Philip returned, then Philip kept his arm around John's shoulders.

"So I guess we caused a ruckus, huh?" Philip asked, giving Marin an apologetic look.

His aftershave, a scent of spiced oranges, filled Marin's nostrils. Clad in tasseled loafers, pleated blue trousers, a white button-down oxford, and a tie with—of all things—grazing sheep marching up and down, he looked nothing like the man who greeted her each day at New Beginnings or rode that blue and chrome motorcycle. She took a step backward, gaining control of her senses. "So he *did* see you."

"And you look like you've seen a ghost."

Marin watched John happily pat Philip's shoulder and beam upward. She stammered, "I–I'm just surprised, that's all. I didn't realize you attended here."

"Is this your home church? Funny I've never seen you. I transferred my membership here about a year and a half ago, but this is my first time at the early service." He straightened his shoulders, his height becoming even greater with the action. His brown eyes sparkled. "I start teaching a junior high class today, so I figured I'd be better off getting here before Sunday school."

Marin nodded dumbly. Well, that explained why Philip hadn't seen John here before. Being an early riser, John had always attended the first service. Because there was no class to accommodate John's special needs, Mom and Dad hadn't stayed for Sunday school. Of course, with Marin away at college, it had been several years since she'd attended this church regularly.

John asked, "Can I go to Sunday school with you, Philip?"

"No," Marin answered bluntly. John in a room full of junior-high age boys? That would be asking for trouble. At Philip's puzzled look, she added more gently, "Remember, John? We go to Aunt Lenore's for lunch after church. So we can't stay for Sunday school."

John pulled a face. "I do not like Aunt Lenore. She is bossy." He signed the word *bossy* with relish.

Marin agreed, but the subject wasn't up for debate. "Sorry, John, but we have to go."

John sighed but didn't argue.

"We could still catch most of the sermon if we head back in there," Philip suggested. He looked down at John. "Want to sit with me, buddy?"

John immediately lit up. "In my special seat?"

Philip looked at Marin, his eyebrow raised.

"The pew in front of the sound booth," Marin explained. "He likes sitting there."

Philip nodded. "Sure, John. I'll sit there with you."

Marin nearly wilted with relief. If Philip were with him, John would surely behave. And Aunt Lenore couldn't complain about John being unattended.

"Come on," Philip told John, heading him toward the doors to the sanctuary. "But we have to be very quiet so we don't disrupt."

John placed a stubby finger against his lips and tiptoed beside Philip. Marin followed the two of them back into the sanctuary. Philip and John settled side-by-side in the middle of John's pew, and Marin crept down the aisle to rejoin her aunt. Aunt Lenore, her face pinched, glanced toward John's pew. When she spotted Philip with him, she gave a brusque nod of approval then turned back to the Bible in her lap.

Marin kept her gaze to the front, but she felt very aware of Philip's presence behind her. She supposed she should be grateful for his assistance with John; yet, if she were honest with herself, grateful wasn't the feeling he evoked.

nine

Monday morning as Marin pulled up in front of New Beginnings, she discovered her palms were moist and her stomach fluttered. And she knew why. Since yesterday, when Philip unexpectedly appeared in the church foyer to assist with John, she had been unable to get him out of her mind. Seeing him at church, away from the New Beginnings setting and his "job," he had turned into a "real person." While she couldn't define why it had impacted her so, she could not deny that she was seeing him with different eyes.

"Come on, Marin. Let's go in." John nudged her with the heel of his hand, waking her from her reverie.

"Um, John," she hedged, wrapping her hands around the sturdy plastic steering wheel, "can you walk in by yourself today?"

John's hazel eyes widened. "You always walk me in."

Marin resisted the sigh that longed for release. John was such a creature of habit. If she disrupted his routine, it might upset his whole day. There wasn't much choice—she'd need to walk him in. *But maybe*, she thought as she stepped out of the car and walked with John to the door, *Philip will be occupied elsewhere, and I won't have to speak to him.*

That hope was immediately squelched with the opening of the door. While Philip did appear to be occupied—he held a clipboard and spoke earnestly with an older, smiling woman—the moment the door creaked, he turned in their direction and broke into a huge smile. "Good morning, John and Marin!"

Marin felt a prickle of regret that he'd greeted John first. *Stop it!* she berated herself. She raised her hand for a quick wave and turned to leave as John trotted across the floor to embrace the woman.

"Marin, wait!"

Freezing, her hand on the doorknob, her gaze on the doorjamb, she waited until Philip came to a jogging halt beside her.

"Hey, I wanted to share an idea with you. I got a request on the answering machine for someone to help out at Barks, Squawks, and Meows, the new veterinary clinic that just opened on Fourth Street, and I wondered how you'd feel about—"

Marin felt her blood pressure climb. All warm feelings toward Philip fled. She spun and interrupted. "Don't even suggest it. Not now, not ever. I've made it perfectly clear that John is not here to learn to go—out there." She flung her hand outward, indicating the outdoors. "He's here to have a safe haven. You told me he could stay for a month, and there's another week left of that month, so don't make any more noises about jobs. Honor your agreement."

While she raged, Philip took a step back and lowered the clipboard to his side, his expression changing from welcoming to woeful to weary. He nodded, his brown eyes clearly displaying regret. When he spoke, his voice was soft yet held an undercurrent of hurt. "Fine, Marin, for one more week I'll keep my silence, as we agreed." He leaned in. "But at the end of the week—then what?"

She had no answer, so she stood in stony silence.

He nodded, as if he knew her options were limited. "You might ask John what he'd like to do. It is *his* future, you know." And he turned and strode to John and the woman, ignoring Marin.

Marin careened out the door, slammed herself into her vehicle, and dashed away as quickly as safety allowed. While she drove across town, her heart pounded and her ears rang. She wished so much someone else were dealing with these issues. She wished she'd never met Philip Wilder, who was entirely too handsome and smart and left her emotions in an upheaval when she needed her world to be quiet and ordered. She wished she could keep driving and driving and driving until she was far, far away.

But whom was she fooling? She couldn't keep driving. She had responsibilities. Her home, Brooks Advertising, and John. Even though she had moments—like now—when she wanted a break, she could never leave permanently.

She pulled into her parking area, shut off the ignition, and lowered her forehead to the steering wheel. Closing her eyes, she prayed inwardly, *Lord, as much as I hate to admit it, Philip is right. I don't have other prospects for John's care. And John should have a say-so in what happens to him. But how much say-so? What can he really handle, God? I don't want to burden him.* The Bible verse displayed on the banner at New Beginnings played through her mind. *What good works do You have planned for John? How I wish I knew....*

With a sigh she raised her head and peeked at herself in the mirror. Her cheeks were slightly flushed, but other than that she appeared composed. Under the surface, however, emotions continued to rumble. If she got busy—focused—she could find a measure of control. That determination made, she headed into Brooks Advertising.

✣

After the morning meeting Crystal followed Marin to her office. She held out a manila envelope. Her expression seemed apprehensive. "Miss Brooks, I probably should have given this to you the first day you came in, but Mr. Ross thought it would be best to wait and give you time to settle in."

Marin pulled her brows down, her stomach churning in sudden trepidation. "What is it?"

"The bank statement for April. Your dad would have taken care of it, but—" She broke off, shrugging helplessly.

Marin nodded, understanding. The accident had changed

many routines. She took the envelope and offered a sad smile. "Well, you're right that I probably should have dealt with this awhile back, but I understand the reasoning behind holding off. Thanks for giving it to me."

She walked to her office, closed the door, and spilled the contents of the envelope across the desk. This distraction was just what she needed to bring an end to her John worries. Pulling out the executive checkbook register, she began the balancing process. All fell neatly into place with the exception of one debit. No reference was applied to it in the register—only the initials R.H. and only a routing number on the statement. She backtracked in the checkbook records, discovering the same amount had been automatically withdrawn from Dad's account the thirtieth of each month for as far back as the register showed.

What is R.H.? she wondered. It was a sizable enough amount to warrant concern. She pushed the intercom button. "Crystal, could you have Dick come in here for a minute, please?"

In moments Dick appeared. Marin gestured for him to sit then swung the checkbook register and statement in his direction. "Dick, do you have any idea what this is?"

Dick examined both documents, his brows furrowed. "R.H.," he mused. "No, that doesn't ring any bells with me."

Marin flipped through the register. "Look. There's a similar notice of withdrawal all the way back to December of last year. I imagine if I check previous checkbook registers, I'm going to find it goes back further than that. But there's nothing here to tell me what it's about. A bill of some sort? Payment on a loan? Do you have any ideas?"

Dick leaned back and shrugged. "I don't know, Marin. Darin always handled the financial end of the business—the rest of us were creative staff, so I can't tell you what it is. But maybe—" He broke off, his expression thoughtful.

Marin tipped her head. "What?"

Dick scratched his chin, releasing a light chuckle. "Well, this might sound far-fetched, but your dad was a strong believer in not letting your left hand know what your right hand was doing. Maybe that R.H. means right hand, and he was making some sort of charitable contribution."

Marin nodded slowly. "Dad was adamant about tithes and offering. He said God gave us much, and as good stewards we should share. You could be right, but why would he keep it so secretive?" She scowled, frustrated. "I made a commitment to carry on Dad's work, but if *my* left hand doesn't know what *his* right hand was doing, how can I keep doing it?"

Dick gave another shrug. "Check with Mr. Whitehead? As far as I know, he was Darin's only legal advisor."

"Yes. . .yes, that's a good idea. Thanks, Dick."

After Dick left, Marin flipped through the file of telephone numbers until she located Mr. Whitehead's number. When his receptionist answered, she spoke briskly. "This is Marin Brooks. I need to schedule an appointment with Mr. Whitehead as soon as possible, please. Would he have some time late this afternoon perhaps?"

ᴥ

Five fifteen. Philip felt his stomach clench when he noticed the time. Marin would be arriving to retrieve John within the next five minutes. After this morning's run-in he wasn't eager to see her. She was wrong. He knew she was wrong, but he didn't know how to make her see it without alienating her. He'd be doing some heavy-duty praying in the next few days to find a way to reach her.

In the meantime, he turned his attention to the older couple across his desk. Their son had suffered brain damage from a severe allergic reaction to penicillin when he was still a toddler. He had always been cared for at home, but as the couple aged they realized they needed assistance. Their initial plea for help had been similar to Marin's, but Philip believed they would be open to a job placement once they realized it would meet their needs.

While he shared the different job opportunities available to New Beginnings clients, he kept one ear tuned to the door. His heart picked up its tempo the moment the knob turned and he heard John greet his sister. But he didn't turn his head—he remained focused on the couple. John hollered a good-bye, and he responded briefly, sending John a quick smile, which also swept over Marin; but then he returned his attention to the man and woman across the desk.

The door closed again, and he heaved an inward sigh of relief. *Can't let her boggle my mind so much*, he thought with determination and continued his explanation to Mr. and Mrs. Jeffers. When he'd completed covering all the work options, he admitted, "I must be honest with you—New Beginnings is encountering some financial difficulties right now."

The couple exchanged a worried glance, and the man said, "My wife and I are on a fixed income—"

Philip held up his hand. "No, no, I wasn't asking you for money. As I said earlier, New Beginnings is strictly non-profit. I do not require a fee from any of my clients. I only mentioned it to let you know I'm uncertain how much longer the services will be available. I want you to know that if I must close, I will do everything I can to find comparable services for your son. I won't leave you high and dry."

The woman's eyes glittered. She pointed to the Bible verse. "Mr. Wilder, did you put that up there?"

Philip nodded.

"Then you're a Christian?"

Again Philip nodded. "Yes, ma'am. I am."

She took his hand. "Then the Lord will provide. He takes care of His own—I know that. All these years He's given me the strength to care for Randy. He guided us here to you when we needed help. He'll give you what you need to keep this wonderful place going. I will join you in prayer."

Philip's heart swelled. This confirmation was just what he

needed. He squeezed the soft, wrinkled hand that rested in his. "Thank you, Mrs. Jeffers. And I'll do whatever I can to help you with Randy."

The couple stood to leave, and Philip walked them to the door with a promise to start working with Randy in the morning. After closing the door behind them, he leaned against it and heaved a sigh.

"Lord, You heard Mrs. Jeffers. She believes You'll provide. I believe it, too. I just don't know how. Would You please hurry up and tell me? And while You're fixing things, please help me find a way to reach Marin."

❧

John sat quietly next to Marin as she showed the bank statements and checkbook register to Mr. Whitehead. "I don't have a clue what this is for, but Dick Ross thought it might be a charitable contribution. Can you tell me what it is?"

Mr. Whitehead gave a short glance then nodded. "Of course I know what it is. One of your father's 'right hand' dealings." He smiled. "You know, Marin, your father was one of the finest Christians I've ever had the pleasure of knowing. His ideas of stewardship would put most of the rest of us to shame. He gave several onetime offerings to various organizations, but this one—this one was extra special. He donated to it consistently for nearly three years."

Marin raised her eyebrows. "Three years? That same amount?"

Mr. Whitehead nodded. "Yes. He fully supported this organization's work." The man shrugged. "Of course, now that you're in charge of Brooks Advertising, it's easily changed. He made the arrangements monthly, so it automatically stopped with his death. It does not need to resume."

"But I want it to resume." Marin leaned forward. "If it was important to Dad, I'd like to continue giving, just as he did. But I don't know who he gave it to!"

Mr. Whitehead's forehead furrowed. "Well, that leaves me

in a rather awkward position, Marin. Your father wanted this transaction kept secret—from the receiver of the funds and from his family. I feel as if I would be breaching a confidence to share the name of the organization."

Marin leaned back, thinking. Was it important for her to know who was receiving the money? She knew she could trust Mr. Whitehead to funnel the money for her—Dad had trusted him unconditionally. While she was curious, it was more important to her that Dad's work continue. She gave a nod, her decision made. "Mr. Whitehead, if you can set up an automatic transfer of funds to this organization without divulging its name to me, I'd like for you to do that."

The man smiled. "That could be arranged."

"I know Dad went month-by-month, and because of that a month was skipped. I don't want that to happen again, so let's set it up for twelve months. At the end of that time period, please contact me, and I'll renew for another year." Marin paused, frowning for a moment. "That is possible, isn't it?"

Mr. Whitehead gave a light laugh. "With today's computer systems it's a simple matter to set up such transactions." His eyes shone with approval. "Darin always spoke highly of you, Marin, and he felt very confident you would continue his work with diligence. It would be easy for you to let this slip aside—no one would ever know since Darin kept it private. I'm proud of you for being willing to follow your father's spirit of giving."

The words warmed Marin. She stood and held out her hand. "Thank you, Mr. Whitehead. Let's restart those transfers on the thirtieth, just as Dad had done."

ten

Philip could hardly believe how quickly the month had flown by. With summer in full swing John had started wearing knee-length walking shorts and sandals in place of the jeans and tennis shoes. Eileen teasingly called him Spanky after the Little Rascals character, and John always responded with a laughing protest—"Oh, Eileen, I am John!"

The two of them were now in the housekeeping center with another client, Bobby, doing cleanup after a session of cooking. Everyone else had left for the day. The mumble of their voices kept Philip company as he paid bills at his desk. He heard Eileen say, "Okay, John, now back to work," and he smiled, certain that right now John was wrapping Eileen in one of his famous hugs.

John knew the routine of New Beginnings so well that Philip was positive he'd be great in a work placement. But Marin remained stubbornly determined to keep him sheltered. In fact, it seemed deeper than stubbornness. There was a real fear. Fear was not of God, and Philip wanted the opportunity to tell her that.

Each day of the past week he'd tried to get a moment alone with her to approach the subject, but she'd managed to sidestep him. She wouldn't be able to do it tonight, though. This was the last day of his stipulated one-month period, so the issue must be faced, and Marin would face it if he had to tie her to a chair and make her listen.

He finished writing a check to pay the utilities bill, scowling a bit as he realized how low his bank account was getting. Before worry could set in, he reminded himself of last night's Bible reading. Philip had sought comfort in the Psalms, and in chapter 32 he'd found it: *"You are my hiding place; you will protect me from trouble and surround me with songs of deliverance. I will instruct you and teach you in the way you should go; I will counsel you and watch over you."*

Nothing had changed. His bank account held only enough funds for another two weeks of full operation. But the psalm promised deliverance. Already he'd found a measure of deliverance. He and Eileen had brainstormed ways to keep providing some services within the confines of his lesser income. Even if he had to use other agencies, his clients would be all right. But he feared he would have to cut two employees because his income would no longer cover their salaries.

"John, the dishes are dry so stack them on the shelf, please. Bobby, use some cleanser on that sink and scrub, scrub, scrub!"

Philip turned an ear toward the housekeeping center, listening as Eileen gave directions. Her gravelly yet warm voice carried over the partition. He smiled, envisioning the scene in the mini-kitchen. Eileen was wonderful with the clients. If he had to drop someone from the payroll, she would be at the bottom of the list.

He slapped his checkbook closed, slipped the check and bill into an envelope, then opened his drawer to dig for a book of stamps. His arm was buried to the elbow in the drawer when the front door opened and Marin entered. He tried to stand, but his sleeve got caught on something, and he flumped back into his seat with a muffled "Ooph!"

Marin covered her mouth with her fingers, obviously trying to hide a smile, but she didn't shield her eyes. He could see the smile in their hazel depths from the distance of twenty feet. The smile warmed him, and he couldn't help but respond with one of his own.

"Yep, caught me in my most graceful moment." He disentangled his sleeve and pulled himself loose. On his feet he rounded the desk and called over his shoulder, "John! Marin is here."

Eileen stuck her head around the partition and flapped her hand in their direction. "John's finishing up. He'll be out in a minute. You two talk." She disappeared again.

Twisting her hands together at her waist, Marin gave a slight shrug. "We probably do need to talk. This is it, isn't it?"

Philip knew she referred to her month being up, but to him the words held a deeper meaning. "I guess so," he said. "Unless something changes." His reply held a double meaning as well.

Marin sucked in her lips, looking up at him with an unreadable expression in her eyes. She tucked a strand of hair behind her ear then gestured toward the stacking chairs in the corner. "Could we sit down for a moment? I—I do have something I'd like to discuss with you."

Philip's heart pattered. He pulled out a chair and set it down. "Here you go." She seated herself, arranging her skirt over her knees. He yanked out another chair and straddled it, facing her, with his arms stacked one over the other on the backrest. "I'm all ears," he prompted.

Linking her fingers in her lap, she offered a small smile. "I want you to know how much I appreciate all you've done for John. He loves coming here, and he thinks of you as a friend."

"I am his friend." Philip leaned forward and added, "Yours, too."

She looked away for a moment, as if embarrassed, and when she turned back he noticed two tears shining brightly in the corners of her eyes. "Thank you." She blinked several times then continued. "It will be hard for me to tell him he can't come back. I know you said one month, and I'm not going to ask you to do this indefinitely, but—as our friend—I hope you'll be willing to do a favor for John and me." She paused, looking at him expectantly.

He threw his hands outward. "Well, what is it?"

She released a light, self-conscious laugh. "I hoped you'd say yes first."

"Can't till I know what it is," he said, his tone teasing. "You might ask me to rob a bank or something."

She laughed again but with less reserve. "Not likely."

Philip erased the teasing from his voice as he encouraged, "Marin, whatever it is, if I can help you and John, I'll do it. Okay? Now quit procrastinating and spit it out."

Marin tucked her hair behind her ears once more—an unnecessary gesture because her hair stayed neatly in place—and drew in a big breath. "You see, I have John on the waiting list of two different day-care facilities, but neither has an opening—yet. I called everywhere after Mom and Dad died"—she grimaced slightly then drew herself up and continued—"but they said all they could do was put me on a list and call when they had an opening. So far no one's called, and I don't know what to do on Monday."

Philip nodded, guessing the favor. "You want John to continue coming here."

Marin nodded quickly, licking her lips. "Not forever. Just till I hear from one of the day-care facilities."

Philip didn't bother to tell her forever might not be possible even if he were willing to continue providing day care for John. "You know my feelings about keeping John cooped up here."

"I know, but as I said it won't be for much longer." Her voice rose with desperation. "Surely someone will call soon."

"And if they don't?" Philip watched her expression change from desperate to defiant.

"Well. . .well. . ." She squared her narrow shoulders and pinned him with a fierce gaze. "Matthew says today has trouble enough of its own without worrying about tomorrow. I'll just worry one day at a time."

Philip couldn't help it. He burst out laughing. "Marin, you are priceless," he finally managed to say.

She didn't look amused. "I'll keep paying you," she said, "just as I've been doing. Will you allow John to come here a few more weeks? Please?"

Philip forced himself to control his laughter. He knew she was not trying to be humorous, but if she could only see herself, sitting so sweetly in a butter-yellow dress with the sun shining on her hair, her little face set with such determination. Such a small package, yet ready to take on the world if need be.

"Marin, I would love to continue working with John. He's a joy—really he is. We all have grown to love him, and I think he's grown to love us." At that moment laughter erupted from behind the partition, proving how happy John was. "But it isn't fair to him to keep him here day after day. He needs new interactions, new challenges to grow. Think about a rose plant that's kept in a closet—it never blooms. It needs sunshine and rain to bloom, which can only happen outside." Philip reached over the chair to place his hands over Marin's, which were now closed into fists. "He'll never bloom, Marin, unless you allow him to venture into the world."

"Outside, roses get trampled. Blooms get battered by the wind." Her voice sounded tight, controlled. Anger was beneath the surface, but Philip decided to forge ahead anyway.

He squeezed her hands and said softly, "But they live to bloom another day, stronger and more hearty from the experience."

She yanked her hands away and stood. "So you won't let him keep coming?"

Philip sighed and rose, too. He looked down at her, his thoughts tumbling. If he said no, she'd have no one to turn to. If he said yes, he'd be enabling her to keep John confined. If he said no, he might never see her again—suddenly a very disturbing prospect. If he said yes, he'd have more opportunities to see her, talk to her, convince her to allow John to spread his wings.

"We'll take it a week at a time," he found himself saying.

Her face lit up. "Really?" The relief was evident.

"A week at a time," he repeated, as much for himself as for her.

She hugged herself. "Oh, thank you, Philip. You are a godsend."

A godsend? Maybe just a big chicken. Sternly he reiterated, "Remember—a week at a time."

John puttered around the corner to give Marin a hug.

"John, say good-bye to everyone. We'll see them again on Monday," she prompted.

" 'Bye, Philip. 'Bye, Eileen and Bobby," John recited dutifully. "I will see you Monday."

Philip watched them turn, hand-in-hand, and head for the door. As Marin reached for the doorknob, he impulsively called out, "Wait a minute."

Marin turned as John went on out. "Yes?"

"What are you doing tomorrow night?" His heart pounded at his own brashness. If he was going to take this a week at a time, he'd better make the most of it.

Marin's fine brows came down. "Nothing. Why?"

He hooked his thumbs in his rear pockets to hide the trembling in his hands. "I thought I might bring the cycle over—take John for a ride, as I promised. And then visit. . .if that's okay."

Marin seemed to examine him for hidden motives. When she answered, her voice held uncertainty. "Yes. I suppose that would be fine."

"Good. Okay." He backed up a step, tripping over one of the chairs. Catching himself, he added lamely, "I'll see you tomorrow night—seven thirty?"

She nodded then slipped out the door.

Philip sank down on the offending chair and buried his face in his hands. A tap on his shoulder brought him bolt upright. Eileen stood smirking at him.

"If you're going to ask a girl for a date, you need to do it with more confidence."

"I wasn't asking her for a date," he blustered. "I just need a chance to talk to her—about John."

"Mm-hmm," Eileen said, her expression knowing. She crossed her arms. "If you'll need someone to stay with John while you take her out, give me a holler. I'd be glad to do it. I'll even bring my cat."

Philip groaned. "Eileen—" But then something struck him, and he jumped to his feet. Wrapping his arms around her sturdy bulk, he swung her off the floor in a mighty hug. "Why, you sweetheart, you!"

"Yes, I am, but put me down!" she demanded, thumping him on the shoulders. He released her, and she continued to grumble, straightening her shirt. But he noticed her eyes sparkled. "What was that all about?"

"It doesn't matter," he said, the smile still splitting his face. "Can you be ready by seven? I'll pick you up—and make sure you bring your cat."

eleven

At 7:25 Saturday evening, the doorbell rang. Marin remained in the kitchen, mixing a pitcher of lemonade, and allowed John to answer it. For some inexplicable reason she felt shy about seeing Philip. She heard John exclaim, "Eileen!"

Eileen? She rounded the corner to see the older woman from New Beginnings step into the living room. A pet taxi dangled from the woman's hand.

John pointed to the plastic cage. "What is in there, Eileen?"

Eileen smiled, her bright eyes surrounded by wrinkles. She angled the opening of the cage in John's direction. "In here is Roscoe the Wonder Cat." She chuckled. "So named because it's a wonder he puts up with me. Would you like to meet him?"

John clapped his hands. "Marin, look! A wonder cat!"

Marin was baffled. What was this woman doing here? And where was Philip? A loud squeak followed by a *clunk!* and *thump!* sounded from outside, and Marin peeked out the window. There she spotted Philip unloading his motorcycle from the back of the most disreputable-looking pickup truck she'd ever seen. She turned to Eileen. "Did Philip bring you over?"

Eileen set the pet taxi on the floor. John immediately crouched in front of it, poking his finger in at Roscoe the Wonder Cat. Eileen straightened and turned her smile on Marin. "Yes. He thought you might like a ride, too, and I said I'd be glad to keep John company." She glanced down and chuckled. "Although it looks to me like he won't be bothering with me at all."

A look at John confirmed his fascination with Roscoe. Marin shook her head indulgently. "Well, I'll go out and check on Philip," she said, knowing she was leaving John in good hands. She stepped out on the porch as Philip put the cycle's kickstand into place.

He turned and grinned. "Will the neighbors complain about having such an eyesore on their street?" He patted the side of the rusty, dented pickup.

Marin laughed. "That's the ugliest thing I've ever seen."

Philip ran a loving hand across the hood as he walked toward her. "Well, beauty's in the eye of the beholder. I happen to love ol' Dixie."

"Dixie?" Marin crossed her arms, unable to squelch a smile.

"Didn't you know trucks run better when they have a name?" He made a face as if to say "women!"

Marin just chuckled. She pointed over her shoulder. "So you brought a babysitter, too, huh?"

"Yup. I figured you'd feel more comfortable going for a ride if someone was here with John. He and Eileen are great friends." He propped his foot on the lowest step and smiled up at her, his brown eyes warm. He must have driven with the windows down, because his hair was wind-ruffled and his cheeks looked ruddy, but it only added to his rugged attractiveness. Marin immediately tried to stifle that thought.

"But I thought you were going to give John the ride," she reminded him.

"And I will. But that doesn't mean you can't take a ride, too."

Marin looked at the bike. She imagined sitting on the back of it, riding through town with the wind teasing her hair, her arms around Philip's middle. Her tummy did a flip-flop. "It does sound like fun."

He gave a crinkling smile in reply.

"Come on in," she invited.

They entered to find John on the floor, his legs widespread. In the V of his legs, a fluffy yellow and white cat lay on its back and batted at a piece of yarn, which John held.

Philip nudged her and offered a smile that set Marin's heart into overdrive. How she appreciated his open acceptance of John.

"Hey, buddy," Philip greeted, "ready for that cycle ride?"

"Not now." John's gaze remained on Roscoe. "I am playing with the wonder cat."

Philip looked surprised, but he recovered and shrugged. "So—is it okay if I take Marin for a ride?"

"It is okay." John jerked the yarn up and down. "You go ride, Marin."

Marin looked at Eileen, who waved her hand in good-bye. She turned to Philip. "Let's go then."

They donned helmets and climbed onto the bike. At first Marin felt self-conscious with her hands on Philip's waist, but after a few minutes she got caught up in the freedom of the open ride—the tug of the wind, the rev of the engine, and the feeling of being one with the cycle. He took a lazy route through town that ended at the city park. He pulled to a stop near the fountain and shut off the bike. It seemed quiet after having the growl of the engine fill her ears.

Philip offered his hand and helped her dismount. She gave a little bounce to recover her footing then removed the helmet and shook out her hair. He put her helmet in the small trunk and placed his on the padded sissy bar. With a grin he asked, "Did you have fun?"

"Oh, yes," she said. "It's a great bike."

He smiled his approval. "Want to walk a bit?"

She nodded, and they fell into step. They walked in silence, enjoying the gentle sounds of a summer evening in the park: children's voices, the quacking of ducks, the hum of locusts. After a few minutes a lawn mower revved to life somewhere nearby, and unconsciously Marin cringed.

Philip must have noticed because he peered down at her with a puzzled look. "Why the scowl?"

"Oh, someone is getting ready to cut their lawn." She gave a slight shiver. "I don't care for the smell of fresh-cut grass."

"But it's the smell of summertime." Philip pointed to a bench off the walkway, and they sat. He turned sideways and bent his elbow, resting his wrist on the edge of the wooden backrest. His fingers hung beside her shoulder, not touching her, but close enough that a slight shift in her position would bring them into contact. The thought sent a tingle down her spine. "You don't like the smell of summertime?"

Marin considered his question. Cut grass was not the smell of summertime for her—it was an unpleasant reminder. Just the thought of that spicy, fresh odor brought forth a wellspring of remembrance, and she tightened her shoulders, willing that particular afternoon's events to be driven far from her mind.

"Marin?" His concerned tone brought her chin up. She met his gaze, and the tenderness in his eyes nearly took her breath away. "You're uptight—I can see it. It seems you hold yourself at a distance from me. Do I frighten you?"

She found the question odd. Who could be afraid of Philip? Despite his size, which could be intimidating, he was obviously a kind, warmhearted person. John trusted him implicitly—but then John probably wasn't the best judge of character. Still, she'd watched Philip with her brother, and she believed he would never do anything to hurt John or anyone else. It wasn't part of his nature. She answered honestly. "No, quite the contrary. I probably trust you more than anyone else I've met—outside of my family, of course."

His smile warmed her from the inside out. "Good." He stroked her shoulder with his pinky finger—one light touch—before bringing his hand away again. She felt a sense of loss with the removal of that simple contact. "Then please tell me what you're thinking about now. I can see something is bothering you."

To her embarrassment she felt tears well in her eyes. She turned her face away to hide. Strong yet gentle fingers cupped her chin to bring her back around.

"Marin, please. I want to help you, but I can't if you won't talk to me."

Philip's tender tone was her undoing. The tears slipped free and ran down her cheeks. Philip wrapped his arms around her, pulling her snug against his chest. His chin on the top of her head, he whispered, "Talk to me, Marin. Tell me how to help you."

Her cheek pressed against the warmth of his shirtfront; her senses filled with the essence of his aftershave. She felt more secure than she'd felt since the day of her parents' funerals. She remained still for several minutes, allowing the comfort of his embrace to give her the courage she needed to share her deepest hurt. Finally, while nestled in his hug, she whispered, "Someone was cutting grass the day—" Her voice cracked, and she swallowed hard.

Philip brought his hands to her upper arms and gently set her aside. He maintained contact by slipping his hands to either side of her neck, his thumbs resting lightly on her collarbone. "The day—what, Marin?"

She took a shuddering breath. "The day everything changed." Marin lifted her gaze to meet Philip's. "It was spring, not summer. Someone was cutting grass, and John was listening to the motor. He said it was a riding mower—the engine was too strong for a push mower. He knew his sounds."

Philip's thumbs drew lazy circles. "What were you doing besides listening to the mower?"

"Walking home. We—John and I—had walked to the grocery store. Mom needed eggs, butter, and bread." She organized the sequence of events in her mind. She pulled down her brows, struggling against the memories. "It was such a pretty day that I asked if I could ride my bike. It was only a few blocks to a little convenience store. But John wanted to come, too." Marin clenched her jaw for a moment, remembering how she'd fussed about having to take him. "I wanted to go alone. As I said, I wanted to ride my bike, and I knew I'd have to walk if John came. He couldn't ride a bike. I didn't want to be bothered with John's poking along."

"That sounds like a typical sister," Philip commented, his sweet smile encouraging. "How old were you?"

"Ten." Marin released a short huff. "Ten, but still older than John. I didn't like having to be responsible for him. He was the older brother—it wasn't natural for me to be responsible for him. I really struggled with it at that age." She dropped her chin. She had never admitted that to anyone before.

After a moment she brought up her gaze and continued, bolstered by the comforting feel of Philip's hands on her shoulders. "Everything went fine on the way to the store. I bought Mom's things, and we took turns carrying the sack home. I forgot about my resentment. John was so happy to be with me—I couldn't stay mad. He held my hand, and then he started singing."

She felt a smile tugging, a fondness filling her chest. "John's always loved fifties music, and he was singing 'Rockin' Robin'—kind of jitterbugging as we walked. I laughed and sang with him. A fun time. . ." Her smile wilted as a chill crept through her veins. "And then John saw the baby bird."

The pain stabbed as hard as if it had happened yesterday. Her nose stung as she fought back tears. "A baby bird—a sparrow, I think—had fallen from its nest. It was under a tree. John saw it first, and he leaned over to look at it." Marin was aware that Philip's thumbs suddenly stilled. "I crouched down to see, too. We were both focused on the bird when we heard someone behind us say, 'Hey, ree-tard, what are you doing?' "

Marin swallowed, and Philip's hands jerked away. His emotional response to her words didn't surprise her—Philip was so empathetic to the plight of people who were mistreated. She didn't look at his face but instead kept her gaze on his clenched fists, which now rested in his lap. "I stood up. There were three boys—probably all John's age—high schoolers, for sure. Two of them stood right behind us;

the third one stood off on the sidewalk, just watching and listening. John pointed at the bird and told them a baby bird had fallen out of its nest. I knew he hoped the boys could help us put it back.

"But the boys didn't offer to help. Instead the tallest one poked his friend and made fun of the way John talked. He repeated, 'A baby biwd,' and the two laughed. I grabbed John's hand and told him we needed to go, but John wouldn't budge. He was too worried about the bird. He asked if the boys would help."

Marin paused, and Philip cut in, his tone stiff. "Of course they didn't help."

She shook her head, pushing her hair behind her ears. "No. They told John to try scaring the bird. Said if he scared it enough it would fly up to its nest. I knew that wasn't true, and I tried again to get John to come with me, but he wouldn't listen to me. He asked the boys how to scare it. 'Stomp at it,' they said."

A sob caught in Marin's throat. "So John did. He lifted his foot to stomp at it. And the tallest boy pushed him. John lost his balance, and when his foot came down—"

Philip's harsh voice interrupted. "I already know, Marin. Don't say it."

Marin lifted her gaze to look at him. His face appeared blurred through her tears. "Oh, Philip, the look on John's face when he realized what he'd done. He was devastated. John would never intentionally hurt anything, and he'd killed the little bird. He covered his face and dropped to his knees. Then he began wailing—a horrible cry. The worst sound I've ever heard."

"And the boys just laughed." Philip's tone was flat.

Marin nodded, affirming his guess. "Yes. They laughed, called John clumsy, said, 'Look what you did, ree-tard. What a ree-tard,' and they walked off like nothing of importance had happened. I wanted to run after them, to knock them down, to hurt them as badly as they had hurt my brother." Her voice quivered with indignation, amazed at how fresh the anger still felt after all the years that had passed. "But I was just a little girl. I couldn't protect John. All I could do was take him by the hand and lead him home. He cried all the way. He cried himself to sleep that night. It was months before he could look at a bird without getting upset again. It was so awful."

Marin swept away her tears. "I was so angry at those boys. They made me feel so helpless. Later, when I replayed the whole thing in my mind, I found that I was especially angry at the one who stood off to the side and watched it happen. I was too small to do anything, but that boy was as big as the others. He could have stopped them, if he'd wanted to. Yet he did nothing. Just watched and did nothing."

She sighed. "So many people do that. They don't actively involve themselves in the mistreatment of people with handicaps, but by their silence they allow it to happen. There are more silent people than those who are openly cruel. What if all those silent people spoke up? Wouldn't things change?"

Philip stared straight ahead, his fingers clutched so tightly his knuckles glowed white.

Marin was touched that he appeared upset. It proved how much he cared for John. She shook her head, finishing her story. "That was the end of John going out anymore, unless Mom or Dad was with him. Mom never trusted people with him again. She kept John close to her for the rest of her life. At least he was safe with her."

"Safe. . .and locked away. Friendly, personable John, just locked away. . . ." Philip's tone sounded as if he'd drifted off somewhere and was talking to himself. Then he seemed to give a start and brought his gaze around to meet hers. "Have you been able to forgive them?" The question came out low, pained.

Marin knew without asking that he referred to the boys. "It was so hurtful. It changed so many things for us. I suppose I should forgive them. It would be the Christian thing to do. But to be honest, no—I probably haven't." She waited for Philip to begin a lecture, to remind her that Christ instructed His followers to forgive just as His Father forgives. Instead he voiced another question.

"If you were to meet up with those boys today, what would you say to them?" His voice sounded strange, hollow. Her story had obviously affected him deeply.

Marin had considered that question before. "If I had the chance to talk to those boys, I would ask why they did it. John wasn't bothering them. There was no reason to be mean to him." A wave of hurt and anger swelled in her chest. Then she shrugged. "But what good would it do? They obviously didn't care about John's feelings. People like that—I guess I don't have any respect for them."

Philip nodded slowly. His face seemed pale, his muscles tense.

Marin frowned. "Philip, are you okay? You look kind of funny."

"Actually, Marin, I am feeling rather—odd. Maybe I should head for home."

Concern immediately replaced the other emotions. "Are you okay to ride your cycle?"

He nodded again, but he appeared to have difficulty controlling his movements. His neck seemed stiff. "Yes. Thank you for worrying, but I'll be fine. Let's go."

Instead of the winding route they had taken earlier, he drove directly to her house and helped her off without saying a word. She watched as he propped his helmet on the backrest and dug in his pocket. He held out a set of keys. "Would you give these to Eileen and tell her she can keep Dixie? I'll ride to her place and get it later."

His change in demeanor caused a lump to form in her stomach. She reached for the keys, but she clamped her hand around his fist. "Will we see you at church tomorrow?"

"Yes." He stared off to the side. "Would you like me to sit with John on his pew?"

What had happened to the warm tone he always used with her? He seemed like a stranger. "Yes, if you wouldn't mind. He's very excited about sharing the best seat in the house with you."

A slight smile—almost a grimace—flashed across Philip's face. "I'm glad I can do something right. . ."

Marin frowned. He was acting so strangely! "Philip?" She tugged at his hand.

He finally looked at her, his brown-eyed gaze seeming to search below the surface, and he opened his mouth as if to say something important. But then his jaw snapped shut, and he pulled his hand away. "Thanks for giving Eileen those keys. Good night, Marin."

The stiff, formal bearing made Marin's heartbeat rise in alarm. Something was wrong. Her voice faltered. "No problem. Thank you for the ride."

He nodded, his gaze now aimed somewhere off to the side. Without another word he strode to his cycle. Leaving the helmet on the backrest, he swung his leg over the seat, started the engine, and roared away. He didn't look back to wave or acknowledge Marin's presence in any way.

His abrupt departure left Marin feeling as if a cold wind had blown around her heart.

twelve

Philip clenched the handlebars of his cycle, resisting the urge to drive recklessly. His heart pounded, the blood rushing through his ears. Tears formed in his eyes, but the force of wind in his face dried them before they had a chance to run. He glimpsed his helmet in the rearview mirror. It spun on the backrest. He should stop and put it on his head. But it was too much effort. He twisted his wrist, giving the cycle a surge that caused the powerful machine to leap forward as he aimed the bike toward a country road outside of town.

Marin's story repeated itself in his brain. He could picture it all—the little blond-haired girl crouching beside the tree, her bulky brother leaning forward in an awkward pose. The intruding strangers teasing, taunting, then a pair of hands applied to John's back. Even over the wind in his ears Philip could hear the anguished cries that poured from John's soul when the baby bird lay dead beneath his foot.

"Oh, why did I allow it?" he mourned, remembering how he had remained on the sidewalk, watching, wishing his brother would just come on and leave that poor boy alone. But Marin was right—he hadn't said a word. Fear had kept him silent. Fear of Rocky, older by four years and so much stronger. He had never stood up to Rocky. How he wished he had. That choice—that choice to stay silent while his brother played a cruel trick—had forced Marin's family into hiding.

Philip was hardly aware of the empty, stretching landscape, the cows grazing beneath a sky of robin's egg blue tinted with pink. Beneath his bike the asphalt rushed by, the faded white center lines becoming a blur as he pushed the cycle faster and faster. But he couldn't escape the guilt that pressed upon him.

If he had stepped forward, if he had tried to defend John, how differently the story would have ended. Marin would have gone home to say, "Mom, some boys tried to hurt John, but another boy stopped them." And Marin's mother would have known that kindness existed in the world—she would have had no need to shut her son away out of fear.

"I'm sorry, Marin. I'm so sorry. . . ." The wind carried his words away. If he said them to her, would she accept his apology? Would she know he was sincere? Would she forgive him? The family had paid the price for his mistake—more than a dozen years of hiding. How could he make up for that?

A hard thud, followed by several tings, sounded behind him, and he looked in his rearview mirror. His helmet bounced two more times before spinning into the weed-scattered shoulder. He slowed the bike, turned it around, then pulled onto the side of the road and killed the engine. Anger billowed as he stomped to the fallen helmet. He scooped it up, sucking his breath through his teeth when he saw the series of deep scuffs left from the sliding ride across asphalt.

Philip ran his fingers over the lines of scratches, his chest tight and tears pressing once more behind his eyes. The helmet would never be the same—forever scarred. Just as he'd left John and Marin—forever scarred inside. Raising his face to the sky overhead, he cried out, "I'm sorry! I'm so sorry for what I did. Please, God—please let them forgive me."

The only reply was the whisper of the wind and the distant cry of a songbird.

Philip pulled his pickup into his designated spot in the apartment's parking area, unloaded the cycle, and rolled it into his storage area. He took another look at the helmet. In the dim light the damage was barely visible, but when he rubbed the back of his wrist against the scuff marks he could easily feel them. He released a sigh of deep sadness then gently placed the helmet on the backrest. After securing the padlock on the shed door he headed to his apartment.

Inside he tugged off his boots and hung his jacket in the tiny entry closet. Flipping on lights as he went, he moved through the narrow foyer to the kitchen. On the counter the blinking red light on the answering machine signaled that someone had called. He considered ignoring it but decided it could be one of his clients. He leaned his elbow on the counter and pushed the button.

"Philip, this is Brad Carlson," came the voice of his lawyer. Philip punched the volume button twice to increase the sound and leaned closer to the machine, his heart pounding. "Good news. I got a notice from the bank today. A deposit was made for three thousand dollars into your business account. Apparently the donor is active again. Thought you'd want to know. I'll talk to you Monday."

The line went dead. Philip stood, relief washing over him. If the donor truly were active again, New Beginnings would be able to function at full capacity. *"You will protect me from trouble and surround me with songs of deliverance."* The words from Psalms replayed in his memory.

He closed his eyes and breathed a prayer. *Thank You, Lord, for this deliverance.* What a comfort it was to know his clients would be cared for and no employees would need to be let go. His burden should have been lifted with this news. Yet he still felt as if a great weight pressed on his chest.

He sank onto a bar stool, covering his face with his hands. What of the problem of Marin and John? The money, no matter how welcome, could never solve that problem. Marin would continue to keep John tucked away, and it was all his fault.

"How can I make it up to them, Lord?" He felt so hypocritical now for the flowery speeches he had made to Marin about letting John go. It had been his action that had sent her family into hiding in the first place. *Well*, he corrected himself, grimacing with the memory of Marin's painful story, *it was*

Rocky's action and my lack of action.

Philip had told Marin he wasn't able to change the past. How he wished it were possible. If only he could turn back time, start that day again, and stand up against Rocky's cruelty. Philip understood Rocky—their father had been a hard, unyielding man who had ruled the household with an iron fist. Rocky had found ways of making himself feel powerful by bullying smaller or weaker children. Philip understood it, but he'd never liked it. Rocky had bullied him, too, and fear of retribution had kept him silent that day.

Suddenly restless, he got up and walked to the window that overlooked the backyard. A streetlight gently illuminated the area. All appeared quiet, peaceful. Philip's thoughts were anything but.

That day and John's anguished response to Rocky's bullying had changed everything for him. He'd never again run with Rocky and his friends. Instead he'd started hanging out with a new boy on the block—David Phelps. David's family had invited him to church, and he'd met Jesus. The Phelpses had become like a second family to Philip, and even after they moved away their influence remained strong. He'd understood the meaning of gentle strength after being with David's father, and he had tried to adopt the same characteristic in his own life despite Rocky's endless teasing.

If only he had met David earlier, maybe he wouldn't have been with Rocky the day he encountered Marin Brooks and her older brother. Philip closed his eyes, trying to forget the fear and desperation in the child Marin's eyes as the bigger boys tormented gentle, unresisting John. Those hazel eyes had looked at him, silently begging him to help, but he had stayed still and silent on the sidewalk, doing nothing. Not even when the baby bird lay crushed and John had fallen to his knees in distress had Philip intervened. He'd merely followed his brother on down the street, on to the Tasti Freeze for a soda with vanilla flavoring—his favorite drink.

He released a mirthless huff. Somehow, after that day, soda with vanilla had never tasted good. Just as the smell of grass tormented Marin's nose, the taste of vanilla soda was like bile to Philip's tongue.

He spun from the window and stood in the middle of the living room, his heart aching, deep regret filling him. He wanted to escape it, but there was no way to get away from himself. The only solution, he knew, was to seek Marin's forgiveness. If she could forgive him, perhaps he'd be able to set aside the memory, to release the burden of guilt and shame.

What had she said when he'd asked her if she had been able to forgive the boys who hurt John? He pressed his memory, seeking her exact words. And then they came, uttered in a pained, hopeless tone. *"People like that—I guess I don't have any respect for them."* People like that—people without compassion or tolerance. That's how she'd seen him that day. The pain stabbed. Maybe she'd see him that way again if she knew he had been the one standing aside, unwilling to help.

Marin had been right when she said there were more silent people than intentionally cruel people. But ignoring a wrong was the same as involving oneself in it—he knew that. He'd tried not to be silent against wrong after that day. He'd vowed never again to stand by silently and watch someone be abused simply because he was different. He'd promised God and himself that he'd make a positive impact on the lives of those whom society often mistreated whether through deliberate cruelty or casual indifference.

The problem was, his determination had come one event too late. He'd been fooling himself for years. It didn't matter how many lives he impacted for good with New Beginnings. He could never change the impact he'd made on John and Marin Brooks and their parents. Nothing would make up for that.

He groaned, drawing his hand across his brow. How would he ever face them again now that he knew what he'd done to them?

Marin sat with John in his pew, watching for Philip. Philip had said he would be here—it wasn't like him not to keep his word. Yet the service would start in only a few minutes, and he was nowhere in sight. John fidgeted, twisting his head back and forth to check both sets of doors every few seconds. Marin knew he was as concerned as she about Philip's absence.

"Philip is not coming," John whispered as the man who made morning announcements stepped up to the podium.

Marin patted his knee. "Something must have come up, John. Don't worry."

John shook his head, his hazel eyes sad. "He is not coming. He will not sit with me today."

Marin's heart turned over in sympathy at his bereft appearance. "Do you want me to sit with you?"

He shook his head.

"Are you sure?"

"You sit with Aunt Lenore. She will be lonely by herself."

It was typical of John to think of someone else's feelings. Marin squeezed his knee and whispered, "Okay. I'll get you after the service." She crossed quickly to the pew in which Aunt Lenore sat. Another couple had scooted in next to her aunt, so Marin had to step over them. She settled herself between the couple and her aunt, leaning close to whisper in Lenore's ear, "Philip didn't come, so John's alone."

Aunt Lenore's eyebrows drew down in worry. "You did tell him to behave, didn't you?"

Marin nodded, irritation rising. Why couldn't Aunt Lenore be sympathetic to John's feeling about being left to sit alone? But she only said, "We talked over breakfast about staying quiet."

"Good."

Surreptitious glances in John's direction through the announcements, chorus singing, and offertory convinced

Marin that John would be fine today. The sadness still showed in his eyes—he obviously felt hurt that Philip hadn't come—but he remained quiet and respectful in the center of his pew.

A soloist stepped to the front, and an accompaniment track began to play. Marin recognized the introductory notes and settled back, eagerly anticipating the delivery of one of her favorite songs. She became lost in the message of the song and almost didn't hear Aunt Lenore's horrified hiss.

"Oh, no, what's he doing now?"

Without asking, Marin knew she meant John, and her heart accelerated in nervous trepidation. She cranked her head around until she could see him in his familiar spot. He was at his pew, but not sitting. Instead he'd risen to his feet, his face turned toward the ceiling, his hands over his head.

Oh, no, John. Please sit down! John's love for music had probably brought him to his feet, but when he became lost in his own pleasure he could forget where he was. What would Aunt Lenore do if he began dancing up the aisle as he often danced through the hallways at home? What would the others in church think? A pressure built in Marin's chest, worry and protectiveness combined.

A sharp elbow jabbed into Marin's ribs, and she nearly leapt out of the pew.

"Marin, make him sit down! He's making a fool of himself!"

Marin swung her gaze quickly right and left. Trapped in the center of the pew, how could she get out without causing more of a scene than John's arm waving could create? Yet disobeying Aunt Lenore's command was out of the question.

The singer at the front of the church broke into a wonderful chorus—her eloquent voice carrying the melody on sweet notes of praise. A glimpse around the congregation showed all were focused on the song. She was thankful no one appeared to have noticed John.

Marin felt caught. If she sneaked out and John wouldn't cooperate with her, they would pull attention away from the ministry of the music. She couldn't decide what to do.

Aunt Lenore poked her again. She gave Marin no choice. Marin turned in the pew, ready to rise; but then she looked at John once more, and her heart nearly stopped.

John still stood, still moved, but now Marin could see that his motions weren't wild actions of improper behavior. He was signing the words to the song! She sat mesmerized, watching as the next verse began. John listened intently, his gold-flecked, almond-shaped eyes alight with pleasure as his hands perfectly formed the heart-stirring words. Suddenly his image was blurred as tears filled her eyes. He was worshipping. There was no doubt.

Marin swept the tears away and glanced at the singer. John was right in her line of vision—was he distracting her? Her serene expression convinced Marin that John hadn't negatively impacted her concentration. In fact, at a small break in the music, she even seemed to smile in his direction.

Behind the singer the choir members all appeared to be focused on John. Marin let her gaze rove across each face. From the sheen in many of their eyes it was evident they were touched. No one looked upset or bothered by John—they seemed to be captivated by his sincere involvement. Tears stung again as Marin realized the singer and choir members were seeing John as she saw him. A great lump of love and gratitude filled her throat.

Aunt Lenore pulled back her arm to wham Marin again, but Marin put her hand on her aunt's elbow and whispered, "Aunt Lenore, he isn't throwing a fit. Look at him. Really *look* at John."

With a moue of displeasure, she swung her head to the side and looked. And her shoulders stiffened. John crossed his stumpy hands, which each formed the letter L, in front of his rapt face and brought them in a wide arc to his sides—*Lord*. His flat face shone with the glory of the word.

"Oh, my—y—y—y. . ." Aunt Lenore's vein-lined hand rested

on her bodice, and Marin could see it quivering—with revulsion, anguish, or embarrassment? Lenore's gaze remained riveted on John until the end of the song.

At the final refrain, John placed one hand on his forehead and dropped to his knees, his head bowed low, his other hand reaching for the heavens.

At that moment Marin heard a strangled sob. Aunt Lenore. She must be mortified beyond tolerance. Marin's heart clutched. Appropriate behavior in church was so important to her aunt. How would Marin defend John after his emotional display had wrought such a reaction from her?

Aunt Lenore turned to look at Marin. Tears coursed down her wrinkled cheeks, but there was no anger or recrimination in her normally icy expression. Squeezing Marin's hand, she whispered, "Let me out, Marin."

Marin tipped her head, puzzled.

"I want to sit with my nephew."

Marin pulled her knees back and allowed Aunt Lenore to step past her. She watched, amazed, as Lenore went directly to John and placed her hand on his shoulder. He lifted his gaze to her, and Marin could see him cringe. But then Aunt Lenore held out her arms. With a huge smile John stepped into her embrace. After the hug the two sat side-by-side on John's bench.

Marin brought her gaze forward again, hardly able to believe what she'd just witnessed. Philip had been right. Somehow, seeing John's response to the song had changed Aunt Lenore's perspective. Somehow it had allowed her to see the John underneath—his tender, loving heart that had been invisible to her all these years. And if Aunt Lenore could change, then maybe. . .

The lump returned to her throat, and she swallowed hard. *Then maybe*, her thoughts continued, *others can change, too*. She could hardly wait to share this amazing transformation with Philip.

thirteen

Philip felt ridiculous crouched behind the partition, listening as Marin greeted Eileen. But he couldn't face her. Not knowing what he'd done twelve years ago. And not after leaving John alone in his church pew yesterday. He was too ashamed to see her. So he remained in his hiding spot, secretly eavesdropping.

"Well, will you tell Philip I'd like to talk to him when I pick up John today?" Marin's voice carried to his ear. He detected a thread of controlled excitement in her tone. "Something happened I want to share with him."

"I'll tell him," Eileen said, her voice firm and determined, and Philip grimaced, imagining Eileen's expression. "Believe me, I'll tell him."

"Thank you. Good-bye, Eileen. Good-bye, John. Have a good day." The door clicked, signaling her departure.

With a sigh Philip straightened and came around the partition to find Eileen, her arms crossed, glowering in his direction. He felt heat build in his cheeks. She held her tongue while John greeted Philip—to his relief John didn't mention Philip's lack of appearance yesterday—and puttered off to the corner with Andrew and Bobby. But the moment John was out of earshot, she erupted.

"Well, isn't this a pretty day when my duties include espionage."

Philip forced a laugh. "Now, Eileen, you were hardly spying on anyone."

"Well, whatever I was doing, I didn't like it, pretending you weren't here when you *were* right here, no doubt listening to every word." She pointed at him, scowling fiercely. "You *did* hear what she said."

Philip nodded. "I heard."

"And you *will* take the time to talk to her at the end of the day. No more hiding."

It was a command, not a question, and for a moment Philip felt resentment. Eileen was one of his employees, not his boss. But he knew she was right—his behavior hadn't been professional, and he would need to talk to Marin. His stomach fluttered so badly he was sure bats had taken to flight within his middle. He gave a brusque nod. "I'll talk to her."

"Good." Eileen immediately dropped her stern pose and stepped close, putting a hand on Philip's forearm. Her entire countenance softened. "Now—do you want to tell me what happened Saturday night on that motorcycle ride? You hardly said two words to me when you picked up Dixie. I have two good listening ears, if you want to make use of them."

Philip offered a smile and patted Eileen's hand. Warmth toward this crusty lady filled his middle, dispelling the bats. The temptation to share his burden pressed at his tongue. But he shook his head instead. Eileen thought so highly of him, had praised his work here so many times. He couldn't bear her disappointment if she knew what he'd done. "Thanks for the offer, Eileen. I appreciate it. But talking won't change anything."

Eileen's lips drooped into a disappointed frown. "You mean nothing's going to happen between you and Marin?"

Philip's brows came down. "What do you mean by that?"

Eileen gave his arm a squeeze and smiled wisely. "You know what I mean. I've worked with you for four years now, and I've gotten to know you pretty well. I've never seen you look at anybody the way you look at Marin. You care for her, you silly man. And I'd bet my last dollar that she cares for you."

Philip shook his head slowly, denying her words. "Eileen, you're imagining things."

She huffed. "I'm not so old I've gone senile. No, you two have the makings of something special cooking." She released his arm and stepped back, fixing him with a stern expression. "But you'll mess it up if you don't repair whatever got broken on Saturday. You can't hide from her forever—she brings John here every day."

"Maybe not," Philip inserted, remembering Marin's message. "She said she had something to tell me—maybe she's found a day-care placement for John so she won't need to come here anymore."

"Well, I'm gonna hope not," Eileen said firmly as she turned and strode away, " 'cause if ever two people fit together, it's you and Marin."

No matter how hard he tried, Philip could not set aside Eileen's parting comment from the morning. All day long he kept wondering, did he and Marin fit? Could it be God had brought Marin to New Beginnings for more than to find assistance for John? He had given up praying for a wife long ago. He'd convinced himself that no woman would want to involve herself and her children—because Philip would want children—in his life's work.

But Marin wasn't like most women. Her experience with John made her different. Her kindness to John made her different. Maybe. . .

But no—he tried again to push the idea away. Once Marin knew of his involvement that April day, she'd never look at him the same way again. It was best to end it now, before his feelings were as obvious to her as they had been to Eileen.

He turned his attention to his ledger, refiguring his budgets. The deposit from his unknown donor made such a difference. July would beam brighter, thanks to the end of his financial worries. He breathed another prayer of thankfulness for the money. Then, curious, he impulsively picked up the telephone and dialed Brad Carlson's office. Once he had the lawyer on the phone, he said, "Brad, thanks so much for getting this donation business straightened out. Any idea why it didn't come through in May?"

The sound of papers shuffling was heard before Brad answered. "From what I understood, the original donor—who preferred to be anonymous—was killed in an accident in late May. Hence he was unable to make the transfer of funds. But his beneficiary—who also desires to remain anonymous— recently learned of the transactions and chose to resume them. According to the bank statement, these deposits are set up to occur the thirtieth of each month until next June, so you won't need to wonder from month-to-month what will happen."

Philip sat, stunned. The word "accident" played in his head over and over. His throat felt tight, but he managed to say, "This is great. But—you're sure you don't have a name? I'd really like to thank this—individual." His heart pounded.

"No, I'm afraid I don't, Philip. The lawyer representing the donor was adamant that it be kept anonymous. Something about right hands and left hands. I don't understand what that meant, but I do understand the word 'anonymous.' I'm sorry. I'll send your thanks through the lawyer, if you'd like."

"I would. Thank you." Philip hung up the receiver with a hand that shook. Could it have been Darin Brooks donating to New Beginnings all this time? And if it were, then that meant now Marin— Philip pressed his fists to his forehead, reeling. That meant Marin was now giving money to the man who had so badly hurt her family. How could he continue to accept these funds from her? And how could he not accept them? New Beginnings depended on that money. If Philip declined its receipt, his clients would suffer.

The event had haunted Philip for years. It was clear to him he would never be free of the consequences of that afternoon's choice.

❧

Marin skipped the final two steps leading to the front door of New Beginnings. The entire day she'd had a lightness in her heart. She was finding her stride as the owner of Brooks Advertising. Aunt Lenore's change in attitude toward

John eliminated the problem of where he would spend his days. Mr. Whitehead had started the contributions to Dad's mysterious charity again, which made her feel as if she were truly following in Dad's footsteps. Everything was falling into place.

And she wanted to share all of these happy thoughts with Philip. She paused for a moment, her hand on the doorknob. Why was it so important for Philip to be the one to celebrate these happenings with her? Her heart tripped. She knew why. Suddenly eager, she swung the door wide and bounced through.

Her gaze swept the area, taking in the neat arrangement of centers and the happy busyness of the few people remaining. Eileen and John sat at a table near the back corner. When she came in they looked up, and Eileen gave a wave.

"Good afternoon, Marin! John and I have been rolling silverware, but I think he's bored with it. He'll be glad to go home today, right, John?"

John nodded, as if in slow motion, then pushed himself to his feet. He ambled across the floor to Marin as Eileen bellowed, "Philip! Marin is here!"

Philip appeared from behind the partition, which Marin knew defined the break area. He approached as slowly as John had. Marin found herself feeling impatient with both of them. This was a happy day! Why did they appear so gloomy?

The moment Philip was in listening distance, Marin began to bubble. "Philip, you'll never guess what happened in church yesterday." She paused, tipping her head. "By the way, where were you?" Then she waved her hands. "Oh, never mind, it doesn't matter right now. You weren't there so John sat by himself, and he gave the most incredible performance of sign language."

She paused to put her arm around John's shoulder and give him a quick smile. He felt warm. "Whew, John, you must have worked hard at rolling silverware—you're all sweaty."

She dropped her arm and turned back to Philip. "Aunt Lenore watched it, and—oh, Philip"—she felt tears form in her eyes—"it happened. She saw John—the real John—and just as you said, her perception changed. It was the most amazing thing."

Impulsively she stepped forward and embraced Philip in a hug of gratitude. She hardly gave Philip time to respond before stepping back and continuing excitedly. "After church we had dinner with Aunt Lenore, as we usually do, and she volunteered to have John spend days with her until I find other arrangements. Isn't that wonderful?"

Philip smiled, but she saw no happy sparkle in his eyes. "Yes, Marin, I'm happy for you. I know you've been concerned."

Marin felt impatience building. What had happened to the Philip she'd known for weeks? A stranger had stepped into his skin on Saturday, and it seemed that stranger still remained. She put her hands on her hips. "Honestly, Philip, I'd think you could get a little excited with me here. After all, you're the one with the goal of changing the world. I thought it would please you to know one small corner of it made a huge change!"

Philip lowered his gaze for a moment, slipping his hands into his pockets and rocking on his heels, much the way John did when he was contemplating something. He finally lifted his head to meet her gaze again, and the smile appeared more realistic. "I am pleased you can count on your aunt, Marin. That's a real answer to prayer. So—when will John start going there?"

Marin shrugged. "I thought I'd let him finish the week here, give him a chance to say good-bye to everyone, and we'd start at Aunt Lenore's next Monday."

Philip nodded and opened his mouth, but John interrupted. "Will my job be at Aunt Lenore's house?"

Marin gave a start. "Job? Well, John—you'll hang out with Aunt Lenore the way you used to hang out with Mom. You'll stay with her and keep her company."

John pulled a face. "That is not a job. I want a job. Everybody gets a job."

Philip seemed to watch this exchange with interest.

Marin gave Philip a helpless look then turned back to her brother. "I don't know what you mean."

John blew out a snort. "Everybody gets a job here! Anita got a job, Lloyd got a job, Bobby got a job—I have not got a job yet. I want one. That is why I am here. To get a job."

"But, John, you'll be with—"

John covered his ears with his hands and squeezed his eyes shut. "I will not listen, Marin! You are not being nice. You will not let me have a job. You think I am stupid. Stupid! Stupid!" He coughed.

Marin grabbed his hands and pulled them down. "John, stop it. I don't think you're stupid." She tugged at his wrists, her voice gentling. "John, please look at me."

John opened one eye.

"John, you know I don't think you're stupid."

Both eyes opened, and he coughed again, pulling one hand free to cover his mouth. When he'd finished coughing he asked, his eyes sad, "Then why can I not get a job, Marin? I want a job, too."

Marin looked at Philip. She saw sympathy in his expression, and she asked for help with her eyes. He must have understood, because he put his hand on John's shoulder and took over.

"John, most of the people here go *out* and work. But you've been working *here*. New Beginnings has been your job all along." John gave him a dubious look. Philip went on enthusiastically. "Sure it has been. You've helped Eileen, and you've helped Andrew. You helped Bobby learn how to load the dishwasher. You've done a great job, John. We're all proud of the job you've done."

John shook his head sadly. "It is not the same." He coughed again, longer this time.

Philip frowned. "Hey, buddy, are you feeling all right?" He turned to Marin. "You know, John's been dragging all day."

Marin touched John's forehead, and her pulse raced in alarm. "John, do you feel sick?"

"I am very tired," he said. His shoulders drooped, and his hazel eyes didn't hold their usual sparkle.

"Well, we'll have to discuss this job business another time. I think you've got the summer flu. I'm taking you home and putting you to bed." She turned to Philip. "He's got a fever. We probably won't be here tomorrow."

"Can I do anything to help?" he asked, his brows pulled down in concern.

Marin shook her head. She could handle things. "Thanks, but we'll be okay."

Philip touched her arm. "I'll say a prayer for John."

Her heart lifted with his sweet words. *Philip Wilder, you are almost too good to be true.* She forced a light laugh. "Might pray for me, too. I'm not the best nurse."

He nodded, his expression serious. "I always do."

Marin thought her heart might burst through her chest. She took John's arm before she did something foolish, like give Philip Wilder a kiss right in front of Eileen and John. "Come on, John. Let's get you home."

fourteen

Marin was awakened by the sound of coughing. She squinted at the alarm clock on her nightstand, her vision blurry. It read 3:04. With a sigh she threw back her covers and padded down the hallway. Turning on John's bedside lamp, she saw his face was flushed. She touched his forehead and cringed at the heat.

John opened his eyes and gave her a bleary look. "I am sick, Marin."

"I know, John. I'll get you some more aspirin." She hurried to the kitchen, got two tablets, and poured a cup of apple juice then returned. But when she tried to get John to sit up and take the aspirin, he turned cranky and pushed the cup away, splashing his sheets with apple juice. His crankiness increased when Marin forced him out of bed so she could change the sheets. She shifted him to the sofa, covered him with a quilt, and allowed him to stay there even after the bed was ready rather than move him again.

She sank down on the blue floral padded chair that had been Mother's favorite spot and watched John sleep. His breathing seemed labored, his chest rising and falling in an abnormal rhythm. Without taking her eyes from him Marin prayed silently. *Lord, please let this illness pass so he can feel better again.*

Philip's words came back to her—his offer to pray for John and his indication that he always prayed for her. Was Philip awake right now, praying, too? The thought comforted her. She yawned, settling back with her head nestled in the corner of the chair. She remembered the feeling of being nestled in Philip's arms on the park bench when she'd told him about the boys who had traumatized John. It had felt so good, so right, to be held there.

Closing her eyes, she imagined the sturdiness of his chest beneath her cheek, the strength of his arms around her back, the gentle way he had prodded her to share her hurt so he could help. Then her eyes popped open, remembering how he had changed after she'd told him what had happened that day so long ago. He hadn't been the same since.

She frowned. She wasn't surprised the story affected him—it was Philip's goal to keep those kinds of abuses from happening to people like John. But why it made him treat her differently she couldn't understand. Yawning again, she realized she was too tired to puzzle it out now. She needed to think about tomorrow, about caring for John. First thing in the morning she would call Dick Ross and let him know she wouldn't be coming in to the office. And she should call Aunt Lenore— she might know of something that would help John feel better. And she'd need to. . .

Her thoughts drifted away as sleep claimed her once more.

%

"Marin. . .Marin. . ."

The word finally filtered through Marin's foggy brain and registered. She sat bolt upright and sprang from the chair then dropped to her knees beside the couch. Touching her brother's hot forehead, she said soothingly, "Yes, John, I'm here."

John tossed his head. "Hurts. . .chest hurts. . ."

Fingers of early morning light slipped through the lace panels covering the picture window, gently illuminating John's features. His lips appeared bluish in tint! Her heart immediately set up a clamor. "Oh, John." Tucking the quilt beneath his chin, she promised, "You'll be okay. I'm going to get help for you. Hang in there." Tears pressed behind her lids as she dialed 9-1-1. "Operator, I need an ambulance. It's my brother—he's very sick."

❧

Philip strode through the hospital corridor, checking room numbers. His chest felt tight as he recalled Marin's panicked phone call an hour ago. Guilt assailed him—he should have been more aware of John's behavior yesterday. John had been droopy, had coughed off and on all day, but Philip had been caught up in his own worries. He had admitted as much to Eileen when he had called her to see if she could man the fort today.

"How could I have been so oblivious? I know people with Down's syndrome are susceptible to respiratory illness. I should've paid more attention."

Eileen had been firm in her response. "Now that's enough, Philip. I spent most of the afternoon with John, and I didn't for one minute believe he was that sick. All the worrying in the world yesterday wouldn't have changed this outcome, so stop fretting." Then she'd added, "I can handle New Beginnings today. You go to the hospital and be with Marin— she'll need your support."

Philip wanted to be with Marin—to be her support. If he was honest with himself, he wanted to be her support for the rest of her life. *But, God, will she reject my friendship when I tell her the truth of my involvement that day?* Philip had determined over the course of the last hour he would not be able to live with himself if he didn't confess it was he and his brother who had terrorized John. If Marin turned away from him, he would have to deal with it, but he wouldn't keep it a secret from her. She had to know.

His gaze lit on number 424—John's room. The door was slightly ajar, and he tapped on it before pushing it open and stepping through. Strange sounds filled his ears—a gentle, rhythmic *whoosh-thump* and a soft whistle. A curtain hid most of the bed from view, but he saw Marin in a plastic chair against the wall, her eyes closed. He cleared his throat. At the sound she looked up, and her white face took on an expression of great relief. She rushed at him, arms outstretched.

"Oh, Philip, I'm so glad you're here!"

He wrapped his arms around her, lowering his head to rest his cheek on the top of her head. It felt wonderful to hold her so close. "How is John?"

Marin pulled back to look up at him, her eyes flooding with tears. "He has viral pneumonia. Most times it isn't serious, but with John. . ." Her voice trailed off. Philip knew what she feared, and he offered another hug.

She pulled away again, and he saw her expression change to firm resolution. "When he's better, I'm going to let him have that job. I haven't been fair to John, keeping him to myself. He's such a special person, Philip—he really is. He shines. Even Aunt Lenore knows it now." She swept away the tears that coursed down her cheeks. "Does that vet office still need someone? John would love to be around animals— he's talked over and over about Roscoe the Wonder Cat, and I think it would be good for him to have something to look forward to."

Philip nodded, pride filling his chest. He knew how hard it was for Marin to let John go. "I haven't filled it. I was hoping you'd come around."

"Good." She nodded, stepping away from his embrace but keeping hold of his hand. "Let's tell John." She tugged Philip around the curtain.

Philip's heart turned over in sympathy when he saw John lying in the railed bed. He appeared much smaller and older. A plastic cup covered his mouth and nose, apparently feeding oxygen. A narrow tube led to his arm, a steady drip delivering fluids and antibiotics. Philip found tears in his own eyes as he took John's hand.

"Hey, buddy," he said softly, and John's eyelids fluttered. "I wanted to tell you something big. Remember how you wanted a job?" He waited for another answering flutter. "Well, I picked out a special one for you. You'll get to be with dogs and cats—you'll like that, huh?" He didn't mention the Squawks part of the services.

Slowly John's eyelids opened to half-mast. His gold-flecked eyes appeared glassy with fever, but a small smile showed behind the mask.

"Yeah, I thought you'd like that." Philip squeezed John's hand, feeling a weak, answering squeeze. "But you've got to get better, okay? The dogs and cats are waiting."

John looked at Philip for another long moment, and then his eyes slid shut. Philip stepped back, turning to Marin. "Poor guy. He's really wiped out."

Marin nodded, her gaze on John. "I know. He needs lots of prayers."

Philip guided her to the other side of the curtain. "I called the prayer chain at church before I came over, so prayers are being delivered right now. Eileen said she would pray, too. I was awake around three, and I prayed for both of you before going back to sleep." Philip didn't bother to explain that part of his prayer was she would find the ability to forgive him.

Marin's eyes widened. "You did? I was awake then, and I wondered if—" She broke off, her face flooding with color.

"You wondered if...," he prompted.

But at that moment the door flew open, and an older woman burst through, her face set in a frown of worry. She descended on Marin, bestowed a short hug, then demanded, "How is he?"

Philip recognized the woman from church—Marin's aunt, Lenore. He listened as Marin answered.

"He's sleeping right now. He seems to be breathing easier, thanks to the oxygen." She shook her head, tears threatening again. "Aunt Lenore, I feel so guilty! He's been rather lethargic and snuffly the past couple of days, but I just thought he had a summer cold. I never imagined—"

Lenore shook her head firmly. "You stop that. Things sneak up on John—always have. Why, your mother would put him to bed at night, thinking he was fine, and come morning he'd be in a terrible state."

"Really?" Marin's tone sounded dubious.

But Lenore nodded firmly. "Really. No sense in crying over spilt milk. He's where he needs to be to get better." She spun and stomped to the curtain. She peeked behind it, gave a brusque nod, then returned to Marin.

"I came over before I had my coffee, and I could sure use a cup." Lenore peered into Marin's face. "It looks as if you need one, too." She reached with a wrinkled hand to caress Marin's cheek. "Now you stop that worrying. God took my sister, but He's not going to take John—not just yet. Not until I've had the chance to really love him." Tears appeared in the woman's eyes, but she thrust out her chin and blinked, eliminating the moisture. Whirling on Philip, she asked, "Who are you?"

Philip held out his hand. "Philip Wilder. I'm—"

"You're the friend John talks about—the one who sat with him in church a couple of weeks ago," she inserted, nodding. "It was good of you to come. Maybe you can talk this girl into leaving for that coffee." When Marin opened her mouth to protest, Lenore cut in, "Now I can sit and watch him sleep just as well as you can. And I'll send out a cry if something changes. Go on—the cafeteria is in the basement. Drink your coffee slow, let it put some life back into you, then bring me a cup when you return."

Marin turned a tired smile on Philip. "We might as well. Aunt Lenore usually gets her way."

"And don't you forget it," Lenore agreed. "Go." She grabbed the chair on which Marin had been sitting and scooted it next to John's bed. She plunked herself into it, her back straight as a poker, and took John's hand. Without turning her gaze away from John's face she ordered, "Didn't I tell you to go?"

Philip put a hand on Marin's back and guided her into the hallway. He released a chuckle. "She's something else."

Marin nodded. "Yes, she is. As gruff as Mother was gentle.

And I never thought I'd have her as an ally. God can do amazing things."

Philip thought about what he needed to tell Marin. Considering the harm he'd done, it might take one of God's amazing miracles for her to forgive him. "Let's go get that coffee," he said. "There's something I'd like to talk to you about."

Philip led Marin to a private corner and pulled out her chair. He seated himself across from her and watched as she doctored her coffee with generous portions of cream and sugar. She looked up and found him watching, and a light blush stole across her cheeks. The blush gave her an innocent look that was nearly irresistible. Her hazel eyes were soft, warm, full of appreciation, and for a moment he faltered in his resolve to confess. He didn't want her expression to change to one of harsh anger.

She took a careful sip and murmured, "Mm, that's good. Aunt Lenore was right—this should put some life back into me." She then tipped her head; concern colored her tone. "Philip, you look so serious. Is it worry for John making you seem so—austere?" Her fine brows came down. "Actually you've not been yourself with me since last Saturday. Did I do or say something to upset you?"

Philip took a draw of his own coffee, giving himself time to collect his thoughts. Although he'd thought of little else since Saturday than telling her, now that the opportunity had presented itself he couldn't find the right words.

"Philip, please talk to me." Marin reached across the table to take his hand. "I hope you know how much John and I have come to. . .care. . .about you. If I've done something, then—"

He pulled his hand away. "It isn't something you've done, Marin. It's something—" He stopped, took a deep breath and began again. "Marin, I'm not going to be able to accept any more money from you—not unless you know the whole truth and can make a decision with all the facts in place."

She scowled, clearly puzzled. "Well, Philip, if John stays with Aunt Lenore or starts working, then I won't be—"

He held up his hand. "Not *that* money. Of course you won't pay me anymore for letting John come to New Beginnings. I'm talking about the other money. The donation."

Marin shook her head, the scowl deepening. "Philip, what are you talking about?"

Impatient, he admitted, "I know, okay? I know you wanted it to be anonymous, but when my lawyer told me the original donor had died in an accident and his beneficiary was continuing with the donations, I figured it out. I'm sorry if my knowing ruins your pleasure in giving it."

Marin slumped back in the chair, her face turning white. "You mean—it was to you? To New Beginnings? That's where Dad sent—?" She stopped, shaking her head in disbelief. "I didn't know."

Philip found this hard to believe. "How could you not know who you were giving money to? That isn't possible."

Marin frowned at him. "It *is* possible. Dad's lawyer told me Dad wanted the donations to be secret from everyone— including you and including his family. When I found he had been transferring funds, I told the lawyer to continue it, but Mr. Whitehead never told me where the money was going. Dad didn't want his left hand to know what his right hand was doing, and I honored that." She shook her head again, her gaze drifting off somewhere behind him. "So all along Dad was supporting New Beginnings. . . ."

Philip could see this knowledge had significant meaning to her, but he didn't have time to pursue it right now. He had something else he needed to tell her. "Marin, look at me, please." He waited until he had her full attention. "Since last Saturday, when you told me about the boys who hurt John, I haven't been able to rest."

Her expression softened. "I know. I could tell you were bothered."

"But you don't know why," he insisted, not allowing her to sidetrack him again. He linked his fingers together and pressed his clenched fists to the tabletop. "Marin, even before you told me, I knew about that day. I can even tell you what you were wearing—green plaid shorts and a sleeveless white shirt with a frog embroidered on the right shoulder. And John had red high-top sneakers with white stripes. Am I right?"

Marin's eyes widened. "How did you know that?"

"I know, because I was there."

Her jaw dropped. "You—you were—?"

He nodded miserably. "I stood on the sidewalk and watched it happen. And I kept willing my brother to *just come on*. But he didn't." He swallowed, unable to meet Marin's gaze. "Not until he had finished his fun would he come on." He heard the bitterness in his own tone. With effort he faced her again. "Rocky was a bully, Marin. And I was afraid of him. That's why I didn't interfere."

"It was you . . ." Marin spoke in a barely discernible whisper.

His fingers twitched with the desire to reach out to her. "I am so sorry. I know how much that day cost you. And if there were any way I could do it all over again, I'd help. I'd pull Rocky away. I'd climb the tree for John and put the little bird in its nest. I'd walk you home to make sure you weren't bothered again. I'd—" He broke off, shrugging helplessly. "But I can't do any of those things because it's past. All I can do is tell you how very, very sorry I am for my part in what happened to John and ask you to forgive me." He paused, seeking some sign of what she was thinking. She seemed dead inside—no response at all in her hazel eyes. He lowered his gaze. "I know it's a lot to ask."

They sat in silence for several minutes. Finally he heard her swallow, and he looked at her, hoping for absolution. But instead she pushed back her chair and said in an emotionless tone, "I'm going to get a cup of coffee for Aunt Lenore and go back to John's room. Thank you for coming, Philip." Then she walked away without a backward glance.

Philip watched her go. Had he really thought he would feel better once she knew? He closed his eyes, fighting tears. *Oh, Lord, how could I expect her to forgive me when I can't forgive myself?*

fifteen

John spent five days in the hospital before being released with the instructions to take it easy for another two weeks. Marin, concerned about staying away from the office for that length of time, had nearly wilted with relief when Aunt Lenore stepped in and took over. To Marin's astonishment their aunt cared for John as if she'd done it for years. The bond between the two of them blossomed quickly, and it was a beautiful thing for Marin to watch.

This afternoon Marin returned to find the two of them giggling together over a game of checkers. Once again her heart filled with gratefulness to God for working this miracle in her aunt's heart. It reminded her of Philip's statement: "When people like John spend time with people like you and me, they discover just how much alike they are."

As had been the case for the past two weeks, each thought of Philip brought a stab of pain. Although she knew he'd been by the house—John always told her when he had a visitor— he had only come when she was at work. He'd made no effort to contact her. And she had made no effort to contact him. She didn't know what to say to him.

With a sigh she laid her purse on the counter by the door and crossed to the table, placing her hands on John's shoulders. "Who's winning?" she asked, forcing a cheerful tone.

John twisted around. "I am winning. Aunt Lenore says I am a checker whiz."

Lenore sent a smile and wink in Marin's direction. "He's beaten me three games in a row. I think that's enough for me." She rose, pointing a finger at John. "You just wait, young

136

man. I'm going to practice and come back; then I'll beat you next time!"

John laughed. "Oh, you cannot beat a checker whiz like me." His chest puffed up.

Lenore leaned down to place a kiss on his cheek then hugged Marin. "There's cold chicken and a tub of my potato salad in the refrigerator," she said, heading for the door. Just before stepping out, she added as an afterthought, "Oh—and that Philip Wilder from New Beginnings needs you to call him. Something about John's placement."

"My job!" John exulted.

Marin's heart began thumping a rapid tattoo. So she wouldn't be able to avoid him any longer. "Thanks, Aunt Lenore. I'll give him a call." Her aunt waved and left.

John stood, wringing his hands with excitement. "I will start my job, Marin! I will take care of dogs and cats. I will be kind to them."

Marin listened with half an ear as John bubbled, her thoughts racing ahead to what she would say to Philip. She felt torn in two. Part of her wanted nothing more than to forget what he'd said so they could go back to the easy friendship they'd developed, and part of her wanted to forget he existed. But she knew neither desire was possible. How could she ever forget Philip—his warm smile, his giving heart? And how could she ever forget that day—that hurtful, hateful day? She sighed. She couldn't.

"Marin!" John's fretful voice broke through her thoughts. "I am talking to you!"

Marin gave a start. "Oh, I'm sorry, John. I was lost in thought."

He frowned. "You are not lost. You are in the kitchen. She laughed, her gloomy feelings washing away. "Oh, John!" She wrapped him in a hug.

He allowed it for a moment then wriggled free. "Marin, you call Philip so I can start my job with the dogs and cats."

Taking her hand, he led her to the living room and pointed to the telephone. "Call right now."

Marin's palms began to sweat. "Don't you want to eat first?" she hedged.

He shook his head, his blond hair falling across his high forehead. "No. I want my job first. Call."

She didn't have much choice. She sat down and picked up the phone. The number of New Beginnings was in her telephone's memory bank, so a push on number 3 sent the call through. John stood nearby, his stubby fingers working against each other in happy anticipation. Marin wished he'd go sit down somewhere.

"Hello, New Beginnings," greeted the voice Marin knew well.

"Hi. . .it's Marin." Her voice came out in a breathy whisper.

There was a long pause and then, equally soft, "Hi, Marin."

She cleared her throat while her heart pounded out a Sousa march. "Aunt Lenore said you called."

"Yes, I did. I have some paperwork that needs to be completed to finalize John's job placement." He sounded businesslike, but not brusque. "Would it be possible to bring it by the house? The sooner it's done, the sooner John can start."

"That—that would be fine," Marin stammered, wondering how she would face him when it was this difficult just to talk to him over the phone.

"Okay. Six or so?"

"Yes—that'll work."

"All right. Thanks, Marin. I know John will enjoy this position." A pause and then, "Good-bye." *Click.* The line went dead.

Marin sat with the phone in her hand, feeling as if something had clicked off inside herself, too.

&a.

The doorbell rang at five after six. "That is Philip about my job!" John crowed and started to get up from the kitchen table.

But Marin held up her hand to stop him. "No, John, finish your dinner. I have to fill out the paperwork, but when it's finished you can visit with Philip, okay?"

John sat back down. It was clear he was disappointed, but he didn't argue. Marin crossed to the door, her stomach in knots, and swung it open. But instead of Philip she found Eileen on the porch. "Eileen—come on in." She couldn't decide if she felt disappointed or relieved by this surprise.

John was far from disappointed. He joined them at once. "Eileen! Did you bring Roscoe the Wonder Cat?"

Eileen gave John a hug, laughing. "No, no, Roscoe is at home, probably snoozing on the back of the couch. I only brought some papers."

Marin frowned. "I thought Philip was bringing them by."

Eileen pulled away from John, her expression grim. "He should have. But that fool man sent me instead." She waved the packet. "I'll take care of this for him, but what I'd really like to do is thump him upside the head a time or two for his stubbornness."

Marin could tell Eileen was gearing up. She touched John's back. "John, finish your supper and then clear the table for me, would you? Eileen and I need to talk."

John gave Eileen another hug before returning to the kitchen. Marin turned to Eileen, gesturing toward the hall. "Should we go to my office?" It amazed her how easily the words "my office" had slipped from her lips—when had it stopped being Dad's office?

Marin sat behind the desk. Eileen plopped the papers in front of her then sat on the small settee against the wall. The older woman crossed her arms and fixed her with a stern stare. Marin braced herself.

"Marin, I've never been one to mince words, and I'm too old to start now, so I'm just going to tell you like I see it."

Marin shrugged. "Go ahead—although I warn you, I can't guarantee anything you say will make a difference."

Eileen huffed. "That's the problem with the *two* of you. You're both as stubborn as mules." A small smile tugged at her lips as she added, "But God planned you that way. Philip needed the stubbornness to be able to break free of the hold of his dysfunctional family and make something of himself. Which he's done, and I'm as proud as if he were my own. You needed the stubbornness to rise above living in John's shadow."

Eileen cocked her eyebrow, peering at Marin with her chin tucked low. "Do you know how many people try to hide the fact they have a family member with a disability? More than you can count, I'd wager. But not you, Marin—and I'm proud of you, too." She crossed her arms. "Stubbornness has served you well, but this time—this time it's hurting you."

Marin frowned. How much did Eileen know? Cautiously she asked, "What has Philip told you?"

"Not much. He did tell me you're our mystery donor. And he said he can't take the money anymore because he doesn't deserve it." Eileen threw her hands outward in disgust. "Doesn't deserve it? That doesn't make sense to me. Philip has done more for the disabled in this community than everyone else combined! New Beginnings is the biggest project, but he organizes Special Olympics events for both summer and winter.

"Somehow he arranged bus service from the Elmwood Towers even though the city council said they couldn't do it because of insurance issues. He runs all over town setting up job placements for people that most wouldn't give the time of day. Doesn't deserve it?" she repeated, losing her crusty edge and finishing on a note of praise. "Philip deserves a lot more than a monthly donation, I can tell you that. Why, he deserves a gold crown!"

Marin sat back, stunned. She had no idea Philip was involved in all of these things. One of his involvements didn't seem to fit, however. "Elmwood Towers?" she asked. "Isn't that a retirement center? Why Elmwood Towers?"

Eileen looked at Marin in surprise. "Didn't you know? One quad in each section has been designated as assisted living for people with disabilities. Philip talked the directors of the complex into making the change about three months ago. Three apartments of each of those designated quads will be rented by a person with a disability, and the fourth will be for the caretaker." Light seemed to dawn in the woman's face. "Marin, that would be perfect for John. He'd have some independence, with someone close by to help as needed, and it would give you your independence at the same time."

Marin held up her hand. "Wait a minute. I'm not ready to—"

Eileen cut her off with a shake of her head. "I know, I know—you're not ready to let the birdling out of the nest. Stubbornness again. But you just watch John as he starts this job—he'll let you know when *he's* ready to be more independent." She laughed softly, her eyes twinkling. "Dear John—he's something else. If ever there was a young man designed to spread good cheer, it's John." She leaned forward and encouraged, "Marin, you should look into it—at least fill out the application."

Marin had to admit the situation seemed ideal—his own apartment, a resident caretaker. She argued weakly, "But we've never wanted to put John away."

Eileen's eyebrows flew high. "Put John away? My dear, you wouldn't be putting him away—you'd be setting him free!"

Marin digested this. It was definitely something to think about and pray about. She brought Eileen back to a previous topic. "Eileen, I want you to know that I'm not going to stop making the donations to New Beginnings, no matter how Philip feels. My father believed it was a worthy cause, and now that I've seen what you do I believe it, too."

Eileen nodded slowly, peering at Marin with lowered lids. "Mm-hmm. Your father started donating—do you have any idea why?"

Marin felt heat build in her cheeks. She'd been considering

that question ever since Philip had told her he was the recipient of those funds. She had a good idea why. Aunt Chris was right—Dad had obviously wanted something more for John. Marin believed he made those donations to ensure the service would be available when Mother finally allowed John to spread his wings. She was so thankful she'd stumbled upon the telephone number for New Beginnings and allowed John this opportunity to grow. *Dad would be thankful, too*, she thought.

Eileen cut into her thoughts. "Marin, I have to tell you something."

Marin raised her gaze. Eileen's serious expression captured her full attention. She nodded silently in response.

"I don't know what happened between you and Philip, and I don't need to know—that's best left between the two of you. I admit I tried to force it out of Philip—got tired of his moping around, and I figured if he'd spill it he'd feel better. But all he said was, 'We've got irreconcilable differences.'" She snorted. "If two people love God and love each other, there is no such thing. You just talk and pray and talk and pray until you've reached a compromise you both can live with, that's all."

Marin burst out, "You make it sound so easy! But some problems. . ." She floundered. "Well, some problems are just too deeply embedded."

"Bosh!" Eileen flapped her hand in dismissal. "There's nothing buried so deep the good Lord can't unbury it and make it right again." She leaned forward to place her hands on the desk and look directly into Marin's eyes. "That man is hurting, but he's too stubborn to come over here, face you, and make it right. So I'm just going to say it straight out. It's up to you. Philip is a man worth fighting for. Don't let him slip away. I believe with everything I've got that God brought you to New Beginnings. God brought you to find help for John, and He brought you to help mend whatever's eaten away at Philip for as long as I've known him. But if you don't do it. . ." She leaned back, sighing sadly. "Well, there will be two hearts that never get to see God's good plan carried out. And that's pretty sad."

Marin lowered her gaze, her mind replaying Eileen's words. *When two people love God and love each other.* Did she love Philip? Is that why her heart ached so badly? But how could she love the man who had been so unspeakably heartless to John?

And it struck her. The man she loved hadn't been unspeakably heartless. The man she loved had been warm and accepting and indescribably kind to John. He had reached out with both arms and brought John into his friendship. He had nurtured and cared for John with Christ's love.

Tears filled her eyes. How foolish she had been. The Philip who had stood silently by and allowed John to be taunted no longer existed. Somehow the experience had transformed him into a man whose heart was big enough to love the ones often despised and rejected by society. God had used that awful experience to turn Philip into the man he was designed to be.

She whispered, " 'The old has gone, the new has come!' " She saw it so clearly now. And, she realized, all it would take was her forgiveness to help Philip see it, too. She looked up to find Eileen still seated, patiently waiting. An idea immediately formed in her head.

"Eileen, thank you for bringing these papers over." She allowed a smile to creep up one cheek, sending Eileen a secretive look. "But they don't make a lot of sense to me. And I'm pretty sure you won't be able to answer my questions. So I think I'd better give Philip a visit."

Eileen hooted with laughter. "Ah, Marin, you are wily." She slapped her thighs and rose, her eyes twinkling. "When I left, he was poring over the books. I'm sure he's still there."

Marin rounded the desk, picking up the packet. "Could you stay with John? It might take awhile to get everything straightened out."

Eileen wrapped Marin in a hug. "Take as long as you need. I'll be praying for you, Marin."

"Thanks, Eileen."

Marin told John she'd be back in a bit, got into her car, and headed for New Beginnings.

❧

Philip sat at his desk, holding a half-eaten sandwich and staring at his dog-eared ledger. *God, I have to give that money back, but I can't see how I'll make it financially without it. Help me out here—open my eyes so I can find a solution.*

Someone banged on the front door. He nearly jumped out of his seat. He glanced at his wristwatch. Almost seven. Who would be here now? The banging came again. Whoever he was, he was persistent. With a sigh he dropped the sandwich onto a crumpled napkin and strode to the door. His heart leaped into his throat when he found Marin Brooks waiting outside. "Marin?" He took a step backward as she charged in. She looked incredibly beautiful with her hair twisted into a loose knot on the crown of her head. Dressed in a Kelly green knee-length dress and high-heeled white sandals, with a soft scarf of green, yellow, and orange looped around her slender neck, she gave off an aura of sophistication without seeming snobbish. Even though her hazel eyes snapped and her chin was set in a determined angle, it was all he could do to keep from reaching out for her. He shoved his hands in his pockets. "What are you doing here?"

She closed the door and wheeled on him, holding up a stack of papers. "I had the impression you were going to help me with these," she said, her tone accusing. "But to my surprise Eileen brought them over." She dropped them on the small table near the door and pursed her lips. "I never figured you for a coward, Philip Wilder, but that's what you are. A coward."

Philip felt his temper building. How dare she stomp in here uninvited and hurl insults at him? Didn't she have any idea how he'd lain awake nights, worrying about how he'd impacted her life? He'd sent Eileen so she wouldn't have to be reminded again of the hurt he'd caused her. He opened his mouth to tell her as much, but she pointed to the chair and gave a quiet order:

"Sit down, Philip. We need to talk."

sixteen

"Now just a minute," Philip blustered, bringing his hands out of his pockets. "You're being awfully pushy here."

"Yes, I am," Marin acknowledged. "I just spent a good half hour with Eileen, and she had a magical effect on me."

"I'm not so sure I like the changes." Philip frowned, examining her from head to toe. Why did she have to be so pretty? Even with that scowl on her face, her attractiveness drew him like a magnet. His feet itched to move forward, his hands twitched to reach for her, his arms ached to hold her—maybe he *should* sit down, he decided. He lowered himself into a chair without taking his gaze off her.

Marin seated herself next to him, crossed her legs, then fixed him with a firm look. "We need to get something straight. And I would really appreciate it if you would just sit there and listen." She paused, waiting for his agreement.

Although he found it difficult to hide a smile—she was too little to pack all this gumption—he managed to nod seriously.

"Thank you," she said primly and lifted her pert chin. "First of all, I *will* continue contributing to New Beginnings, just as my father did. Dad knew a worthy cause when he saw one. I've had some time to consider why he wanted it kept secret, and I think it's because he didn't want Mom to feel as if he were forcing her to do something she didn't want to do. Dad always let Mom have the lead with John. But I think, deep down, he hoped the program would be around long enough to be of benefit to his son." She paused for a moment, her hazel eyes shining brighter with the tears that suddenly appeared in their corners. "And it has been."

She sniffed, shifted the knot of her scarf higher on her

shoulder, and went on. "Second, if John is going to take this position with"—she consulted the paper—"Barks, Squawks, and Meows, he's going to be under your jurisdiction, which means we'll be running into each other from time to time. And this—evasion—just won't work."

Philip couldn't let that go. "Now, Marin, I'm not the only one who's been practicing evasion."

She had the good grace to blush. For a moment she dipped her head, her bluster fading, but then she popped back up and came at him again. "I know, but you've been by the house three times since John got out of the hospital, and every time you chose an hour of day when you knew I wouldn't be there. I haven't had any reason to come to you, till now, so you're the *bigger* evader."

"In more ways than one," he quipped.

A smile flashed through her eyes, but she pointed at him and admonished, "Don't try to be cute. And I told you not to talk."

"Yes, ma'am." He saluted her, biting down on the insides of his mouth to keep from laughing.

She frowned severely then went on. "Last, but certainly not least, is the issue of—" Suddenly her expression changed from sternness to great remorse. The tears that had made an earlier appearance recurred to spill down her cheeks in a silvery trail. Her fingers trembled she swept them away, but her gaze never left Philip's face.

He held his breath, wanting to take her in his arms, but fearful of how she'd react. So he pressed his palms against his thighs and waited for her to gain control.

Finally she spoke in a tremulous tone. "Last is the issue of your apology. And how wrong I was not to accept it the moment it was offered."

Philip's heart pounded in double-time. "Marin—"

"No, let me finish." She swallowed and leaned forward slightly. "I realized something. I've always seen that day as the day everything changed, and I always saw it as a negative. But it wasn't all a negative change, Philip. Look at everything you've done because you saw the suffering of one boy and his little sister! Look at all the good that has come out of it."

She gestured to indicate their setting, a single strand of hair slipping free to frame her cheek. "Philip, I could hardly believe it when Eileen told me everything you've done for the disabled in this community. Your whole adult life you've been giving so people with disabilities can lead more productive, happier lives. Would you have chosen that route had it not been for an April day and a baby bird and a brother and sister who felt helpless against a bully? Answer me—would you?"

Philip sat thinking about the question. In all honesty, he realized, probably not. The event had been the impetus that drove him away from Rocky's influence and straight into the friendship with David, whose influence had been so much more positive. In all likelihood he would have continued trailing after Rocky, living in his shadow, never discovering the joy of knowing God and giving back to Him. Slowly he shook his head.

She beamed through her tears. "So don't you see? As hard as it was, God has used it to bring you toward your perfect plan." She pointed to the verse displayed above their heads. "You have become God's workmanship, performing the good work He planned for you."

"But what about you and John?" Philip demanded. "How has any of this been for your good?" The guilt stabbed again, the memory of John's cries and Marin's grief-stricken face surfacing once more to haunt him.

"I don't know." Her honesty surprised him. Then she flipped her palms outward. "But who am I to question? Maybe there was a good, but we missed it. Maybe Dad was remembering that day when he decided to help get your business up and running. Maybe it was Dad's contribution that kept your business running long enough for me to find you when I needed you. Maybe. . ." Her voice drifted off, and she gave a delicate shrug. "Maybe I won't know until I get to heaven. Some things are like that—mysteries until we're at His side, and then we'll know."

Philip felt tears sting behind his nose as Marin continued softly.

"But I do know this. You've made a difference in John's life and in mine. And I can never regret making the phone call that connected me with you." Her chin quivered. "Philip, whatever happened that day twelve years ago has been more than made up for with what you've given to John and me. You've given me the confidence to allow John to step out and become his own person. You've given John the opportunity to reach out. And I'm sorry I didn't say so at the hospital. I know I hurt you with my silence. I was just so confused and worried."

He finally gave in to his feelings and leaned forward, taking her hands. "I know. I understand. When I think about what I did—what I didn't do—I was so wrong."

Marin's eyes shone as she tugged on his hands. "But don't you see, Philip? You aren't the same person who stood there and did nothing. The old Philip has passed away; the new Philip is a man determined to do good. You've made so many things new for so many people. I admire you for that."

"Then"—he hardly dared to ask—"does this mean you've forgiven me?"

Her response came so quickly it left no doubt in Philip's mind of her sincerity. "A million times over."

His heart lifted. The burden of guilt seemed to leap from his shoulders. A smile burst on his face as if of its own volition. "Thank you."

"No," Marin corrected, turning her hands to link fingers with him. "Thank *you*. Thank you for becoming who you are. And thank you for helping me become who I needed to be for John."

They sat in silence, hands linked, while the clock on the wall counted off the seconds and their hearts pattered in offbeats with the intruding tick-tick. At long last Philip released a sigh and asked, "May I speak now?"

Marin giggled, dropping her gaze. When she raised her head again, her expression appeared self-conscious. "I must have sounded like a real harpy, ordering you around like I did. But it was the only way I could find the courage to get it all out."

Warmth flooded Philip's chest. "Don't ever be afraid to tell me what you think, Marin. I. . .care about you. . .and your feelings. You don't ever have to be afraid with me."

She nodded, her gaze locked with his. "I know. And I'm not afraid."

"Good." He squeezed her hands before releasing them and rose. Amazing how good it felt to know he'd been forgiven. The knot of sorrow that had filled his belly for the past two weeks fled. And suddenly he wanted something more than the cold sandwich turning crusty on his desk. He slapped his tummy. "I'm hungry. Have you had supper?"

She stood up, laughing. "That was an abrupt change in subject."

"Sorry, but my stomach growled. So—have you?"

"Yes, actually Aunt Lenore had supper ready when I came home tonight."

Philip grinned at her. "You know, I've gotten to where I like that lady. Spunky. Tells it like it is."

Marin gave him a sidelong look. "And what exactly has she told you?"

He threw back his head and laughed, delighted to be teasing with her. "Oh, no, that's none of your concern." He ignored her hands-on-trim-hips pose and interjected, "So do you want to go get an ice cream or something and watch me eat?"

Marin hesitated, and for a moment Philip's chest felt tight.

She finally answered. "I left John with Eileen, but I didn't plan to be gone so long."

Philip shrugged. "Then let's get John. He likes ice cream, too."

Marin looked at him uncertainly. "Are you sure?"

Philip reached out to touch her soft cheek with his knuckles. "Marin, I like John. Spending time with him is not a trial." He dropped his hand. "So—what are we doing?"

Marin smiled. "We're going for ice cream."

Philip snatched up the papers she'd dropped earlier. "Afterward I'll come in, and we'll fill these things out, okay? I think John's ready for his job."

"I think John's ready for *life*."

◆

Philip insisted that Eileen join them for ice cream, too, rounding out the group. John licked his cone happily while the other three adults visited. Midway through her sundae, Eileen fixed Philip with a guarded look and announced, "I'm going to tell you something while I have protection."

"Protection?" he queried, leery of the expression in her eyes.

"Yep." Eileen pointed her thumbs at John and Marin. "These two. You like them too much to cause a scene in front of them."

Philip suspected he wasn't going to like what he was about to hear. "Well, as you're so fond of saying, spill it."

Eileen pushed her plastic spoon into the mound of ice cream and followed his directive. "Philip, I've worked for you since New Beginnings opened, and I've loved it—most every minute of it. But I have to be honest—lately I've wondered if I need to make a change."

The unease in Philip's belly grew. "What do you mean, a change?"

Eileen frowned at the interruption. "I grow attached to the clients, and then they march out the door, and it's hard on my old heart to say good-bye over and over again. Maybe I need a place to work where I won't have to go through that constant letting go process." Her expression softened. "I said good-bye to my husband ten years ago, Lord bless him. All my kids trooped off to other states to start their own lives, and I only see them on holidays. I need connections with people—connections that aren't always going to be leaving me behind."

"Are you quitting?" Marin asked the question.

"Yes, I think I am."

Philip shook his head. "But, Eileen, what will I do without you? You're my right-hand man."

John looked up, his eyes wide. "Philip, you have made a mistake. Eileen is a lady."

Eileen patted John's arm, chuckling indulgently. "It's just an expression, John—he knows I'm a lady." Then she turned back to Philip. "A lonely lady, Philip. I want to find—well, a surrogate family that isn't going to outgrow me every six to ten weeks." She took in a deep breath. "So—I've applied at Elmwood Towers to be an assisted living caretaker. That should meet my desire to be needed and give me somebody to fuss over. But"—she gave him a pleading look—"I'll need a good recommendation from my former boss."

Although it pained Philip to think of Eileen leaving, he loved her too much to hold her back if this was what she wanted. He reached across the table and placed his hand over hers. "You'll get it. I'll miss you, but I understand. I can't think of anyone better for the job."

John crunched the last of his cone and spoke around the remnants. "I will have a job now, too. And I will be the most better at my job. Right, Eileen?"

Eileen put her arm around John's shoulders and gave a squeeze. "That's right, John. You will be terrific with the cats and dogs at Barks, Squawks, and Meows."

John beamed.

Eileen lowered her eyelids and looked at Marin although

Philip believed her words addressed John. "And maybe, just maybe, we'll see each other again."

"Maybe, Eileen," Marin responded in a thoughtful tone.

Philip glanced back and forth between the two women, taking in their expressions. Obviously secret messages were being exchanged.

"Oh, I will see Eileen," John inserted confidently. "You will bring Roscoe the Wonder Cat to Barking Squawking Meows, and I will take care of him."

Eileen laughed. "That sounds good to me." She looked at Philip again, and her faded blue eyes softened. "I hope to stay in touch with you, too, Philip. You're a connection I don't want to lose."

Philip realized in that moment how much Eileen meant to him. She'd become more than a friend—he'd come to depend on her in the absence of his mother, who had died more than ten years ago. In many ways Eileen had been more available and loving than his mother had been. "You can count on that," he assured her. "You're my sounding board and advice-giver. Won't last long without you."

She gave him a smile then yawned. Glancing at her wrist-watch, she exclaimed, "Is it after nine already? Poor Roscoe—I've got to get home." She rose, sent a hurried good-bye around the table, then rushed out.

Philip turned to Marin and sighed. "Well—I guess we should head out, too. We still have that paperwork to complete."

Marin nodded, scooping up her purse. "Yes. If John's going to be the 'most better,' we need to let him get started."

"Hurray!" yelled John.

And Philip noticed that Marin didn't even cringe when people turned to stare.

seventeen

The third Monday of September, Philip stepped into the cool interior of Barks, Squawks, and Meows. A whirring fan overhead stirred the scent of cinnamon—a scent chosen, no doubt, to mask the odors of animals and antiseptic. He smiled, taking in the wallpaper that showed cartoon cats and dogs raining from the heavens. Black paw prints were painted on the floor, guiding him to the receptionist counter, which was constructed to resemble a pile of dog biscuits. He chuckled to himself, thinking how the fun-spirited décor matched the whimsical title of the veterinarian's office.

He passed rows of benches where customers waited their turn with the doctor, each person holding a small cage or a leash. Offering a nod of hello to the clients, he crossed to the counter and greeted the receptionist. "Hi, Nancy."

Nancy looked up from the computer and offered a bright smile. "Philip! Here to check on John?"

Philip nodded. He leaned on the counter. "Yep. How's he working out?"

Nancy laughed. "He's a character, that's for sure. Just settled in and made himself at home. He never complains about anything we give him to do, he's great at following directions, and he loves the animals. I'd say you found a perfect match for us."

Philip wasn't surprised by this news. He'd had a feeling John would fit in here. Dr. Powers and his wife, Nancy, were the kind of sponsors Philip preferred—kind, Christian, patient people who offered a warm, accepting working environment. "I'm glad to hear that."

"Larry has the evaluation all filled out for you," she added, flipping through a stack of papers next to the computer keyboard. She frowned. "I had it a minute ago." She looked at another stack then sighed. "It's been a zoo this morning. It might take me awhile to locate it. Why don't you go back and say hi to John? Larry's got him cleaning kennels—just follow the barks."

Philip laughed and pushed off from the counter. "Thanks— I'll be back in a bit." He headed out the side door and followed the sidewalk around the back of the office where a long row of fenced kennels stood. As he passed the tall cages, the dogs barked their greetings, jumping against the chain link to welcome him with lolling tongues and wagging tails. He reached through the openings in the fence to scratch a few ears as he made his way to the farthest kennel, where he finally located John.

"Hey, buddy!" he hollered over the sound of the barks.

John held a water hose, spraying the concrete floor of the kennel. At Philip's greeting he turned his head, and his whole face lit up with happiness. He dropped the hose, splattering his shoes, and rushed to the end of the kennel to wrap his fingers around the chain link. "Philip! What are you doing at Barking Squawking Meows?"

Philip hid a smile. John would never get the name right. "Came to see you," he answered, "to make sure you're okay. How's it going?"

"It is going good." John's almond-shaped eyes shone. "I like this job. I like Dr. Larry. I like Nancy. I like the dogs and the cats. They like me, too."

Philip nodded. "I'll bet they do."

John's face clouded for a moment. "Sometimes the dogs and cats have to get shots, and that makes them sad. But then Dr. Larry lets me pet them. That makes them feel better again."

"I'm sure they appreciate your petting them, John," Philip assured him.

"Are you coming for supper tonight? Marin is cooking

hamburgers on the grill." In his excitement John signed the words as he spoke. "And we baked a chocolate cake, too. Are you coming?"

Philip smiled. He'd been eating more meals with John and Marin than he ate at his own place lately. But he couldn't decline the invitation. "I'd like to. Are you sure it's okay with Marin?"

"Marin said the way to a man's heart is through his stomach, and she will bake cakes every day for you."

Philip laughed. There were no secrets with John. He wondered how Marin would like it if she knew what John had just shared. "Then I'll be there," he said. "I have to go now. Have fun."

"Okay. 'Bye, Philip." John turned and retrieved the hose. He went back to spraying, a look of concentration on his face.

Philip headed back to the office, chuckling to himself. He knew that the first few days here had been unpleasant for John. A couple of high school boys who came in after school had given him a hard time, convincing him to do their jobs and teasing him. But Dr. Larry had made it clear that type of behavior was unacceptable then gave the boys the option to straighten up or find another place to work. One of the boys had immediately quit, but the other—Andy—had promised to change his attitude. Since then, Andy and John had formed a friendship. John had invited him to church, and Andy was attending regularly. It gave Philip's heart a lift to see the positive influence John had made on that young man.

Nancy had uncovered the evaluation, which she handed to Philip, and he left with a reminder to call if any problems arose. As he drove through town toward New Beginnings, his thoughts drifted across all of the changes that had occurred in John's life—and consequently Marin's—over the past several weeks.

Four weeks earlier he had used Dixie to help Marin move John into an apartment at Elmwood Towers right across the hall from Eileen's. While he and Marin arranged the furniture taken from John's bedroom and the Brookses' basement rec room, John had wandered the halls, greeting his new neighbors and letting them know they were welcome to visit anytime.

Her first night without her brother at home, Marin had called Philip and mourned for nearly an hour, certain she had done the wrong thing—John would never survive, he would feel abandoned, he would resent being forced from his home. The second night she had called to confess John was fine with the new arrangement, but she missed him terribly and wished Eileen had never mentioned the idea, and how would she bring him home without making him feel as if he had failed? But the third night's call had been full of cheerful self-deprecation—"I'm the most over-protective, self-centered sister in the world. John *loves* his apartment and his freedom. How could I even *think* of telling him to come home again?"

Letting go of John had helped Marin trust that no matter where John was, God was with him, and she could let him go without fear. Philip knew how difficult the letting-go process had been, and he admired her for putting John's needs ahead of her own.

Those three nights of calls had started a habit of daily communication, which Philip eagerly anticipated. His friendship with her had blossomed until he couldn't imagine what he would do without it. Increasingly his thoughts turned toward the future and making Marin a permanent part of his life. But as yet he hadn't found the courage to tell her.

John still ate all of his evening meals with Marin, at her insistence. She picked him up from work each afternoon then took him to his apartment midevening. She had confided to Philip it would be hard when the time change and weather conditions forced her to end the ritual. But if Philip were honest with himself, he looked forward to it. Perhaps he'd have an evening completely alone with Marin. Maybe then he'd find the ability to speak the words that hovered on his heart: *I love you, Marin. Marry me.*

৯

As Marin drove toward the veterinarian's office to retrieve John, she looked ahead to the evening's cookout—probably the last one of the year since fall was nearly upon them. She'd confirmed Aunt Lenore and Eileen were coming, but she hadn't reached Philip. When she'd called New Beginnings he had been out, and apparently the person who took the call hadn't given him the message because she hadn't heard from him. She sighed. Although there would be plenty of company, she knew she would miss Philip's presence. She admitted things felt lonely unless Philip was there, too.

When, she wondered, had her relationship with him taken on such meaning? It had crept up on her, much like the sunrise—starting soft and pink and dreamy, then growing to beam bright yellow and strong. Her heart filled as she thought of everything he had done for her and John. Philip was such a special man—a special, loving, giving, tender man, and she wished she could find a way to tell him without making a fool of herself. For wasn't it the man's responsibility to make the first move? But what if he never did? What if the guilt he carried from the past—the remembrance of that day—forever kept him from proclaiming his feelings for her? What then?

She pulled into the parking area of Barks, Squawks, and Meows and waited. After only a minute or two John ambled out and climbed in, his face glowing. He leaned across the seat to give Marin a kiss then fastened his seat belt.

"Phew, John. You smell like a wet dog." Marin softened the complaint with a smile as she turned the car toward home.

John grinned, not at all insulted. "I have been with a wet dog. He was scared after I accidentally watered him with the hose. So I held him and let him know I was sorry."

Marin's heart expanded at John's tender concern for all creatures. "I'm sure he appreciated it."

"Oh, yes. He licked my hand." John signed, "All is forgiven." Then he turned to Marin, his eyes wide. "Oh! Philip came today"—Marin's heart leapt at the mention of that name—"and I told him come eat a hamburger and cake so you could get to his heart through his stomach."

Marin nearly drove the car onto the sidewalk. "You told him *what?*"

John scratched his head. "I said what you said. You said the chocolate cake was because the way to a man's heart is through his stomach."

"You *told* him that?" Marin clutched the steering wheel with both hands. She couldn't decide whether to laugh or cry. "Oh, John!"

"What?" John's tone showed his puzzlement.

"I didn't mean for you to repeat that." Her face felt hot. She turned up the air conditioning even though the car was comfortably cool. "John, you can't go around repeating everything I say."

"I do not repeat everything you say," he said defensively. "I cannot remember everything you say."

Despite her embarrassment Marin couldn't hold back a hoot of laughter. "Oh, John," she repeated, but her tone bubbled with humor.

They visited cheerfully the rest of the way home; then Marin put John to work cutting up celery and carrots for a relish tray. By six her guests began to arrive—Eileen first, carrying a platter of aromatic, homemade onion rings, then Aunt Lenore with her famous potato salad. Philip came last. With a bouquet of yellow roses and daisies and a smile that went straight to Marin's heart.

The evening passed in a pleasant time of camaraderie, and although Marin enjoyed each minute, she could hardly wait for everyone to leave so she could give Philip a private thank-you for the flowers. Philip came along when she drove John to his apartment, and of course they had to walk up with him and visit for a few minutes. Impatience tugged at Marin's chest—when would she and Philip be alone? Finally John yawned and indicated a readiness for sleep.

"Lock your door," Marin admonished as she kissed him good night. "And I'll see you tomorrow. Call me if you need anything."

"I know, I know," John grumbled, pushing her out the door. "You are a worrywart." He shut the door in her face.

Marin waited until the lock clicked before she turned to Philip with a shrug. "I guess John's doing okay on his own."

Philip smiled. "I guess John's doing *great* on his own." They started toward the elevator. "And so are you."

"Yes," she mused, "I suppose so." But did she always want to be on her own? Of course not. She wanted her own family—a husband, children, maybe a dog. But she kept silent.

❧

They crossed the parking lot beneath a star-studded sky. Philip stretched out his hand to capture hers. When she looked up at him, he explained lamely, "It's dark—I don't want you to stumble."

She smiled and gave his hand a squeeze that sent a jolt of reaction clear to his midsection. They reached the car, and he opened her door for her then climbed in on the opposite side. His knees nearly touched his chin, his lanky frame much too long for the seating area of the compact car.

Marin laughed at him as she started the engine. "You really don't fit in here, do you?"

He gave her a sidelong glance. In the muted light from the dashboard her eyes took on a deeper hue, her blond hair turning honey brown. He found himself saying, "I don't fit too well in your car—but how about in your life?"

He watched as her hand froze on the gearshift and her face flooded with color. "M—my life?"

He nodded. Reaching across the console, he took her hand. "Marin, I've been trying to tell you something for weeks, but I can't ever seem to find the right words. I tried to tell you tonight with the flowers." He paused. "Do you know the meanings behind yellow roses and daisies?"

She pushed silken strands of hair behind her left ear. "No one's ever given me flowers before."

Philip raised his eyebrows. "A pretty girl like you? You've never gotten flowers?"

Marin shook her head. "Most boys. . .well, once they met John. . ." Her voice trailed off as she gave a slight shrug. "I never dated much—too many other things to take care of."

He made a mental note to bring her flowers once a week, at least. Rubbing his thumb over her knuckles, he explained, "The yellow roses stand for friendship. Our friendship is so important to me, Marin. I've learned to trust you, confide in you, and rely on you. You're my best friend."

Her hazel eyes took on a softness. She whispered, "I feel that way about you, too."

He smiled, his heart swelling. He went on. "And the daisies have several meanings—innocence, purity, and loyal love. I believe all three of those fit you perfectly. I especially admire the loyal love you bestow on John. The relationship you two share is unique and special, Marin. I envy it."

She tipped her head, her expression pensive. "Philip, do you ever see your brother?"

Philip lowered his gaze. The thought of Rocky brought a rush of unhappy remembrances. He shook his head, his heart heavy.

"Don't you think you should?" she prodded. "Family is so important—and he's all you have. You're all he has. You should try to build a relationship with him."

Philip knew Marin didn't understand all the idiosyncrasies of his disjointed family. He suspected even if she did know, she'd still encourage him to try to be Rocky's brother in the true sense of the word. Apparently he remained silent too long, because she pulled her hand free to shut off the ignition and open the glove compartment. She removed a small New Testament and snapped on the overhead light.

Flipping pages, she asked, "Philip, remember when I told you the old Philip was gone and you had become new?"

He nodded.

She held the open Testament to him. "I didn't come up with it myself. Read verses 17 and 18 of 2 Corinthians 5."

Obediently he took the book and held it up to the light. It wasn't an unfamiliar text, but he was curious why she'd chosen it. When he'd finished he looked at her.

Intently she met his gaze. "I wanted you to read verse 18, too, because it speaks of reconciliation. Awhile back Eileen told me you'd said irreconcilable differences had come between us, but she said God could fix anything if you pray and talk and pray and talk."

She reached for his hand, and he linked fingers with her, her palm warm against his. "Philip, God took the old thing from our past and created something new and beautiful out of it. He can do the same thing for you and Rocky, if you'll pray about it and give Him a chance."

Philip considered her words. She was right that he'd believed the event from their past would forever hold them apart. Yet forgiveness had let them bridge the gap, reconciling their friendship. Maybe there was hope for building a relationship with Rocky. He closed the New Testament, returned it to the glove box, then turned to Marin once more.

"Would you be willing to go with me when I talk to my brother? I've met most of your family—maybe it's time you met what's left of mine."

Marin didn't hesitate, which proved the changes that had taken place in her heart. "Of course I'll go. And I'll pray for a reconciliation and a brand new start for the two of you."

Philip had never loved her more.

❧

Nearly a month passed before Philip was able to arrange a get-together with Rocky. Rocky had insisted they meet at a restaurant on the outskirts of town—he didn't want Philip in his neighborhood. So Philip picked up Marin in his beloved, battered Dixie truck, and together they joined his brother at Pete's BBQ, a dim, smoky hangout with which Rocky seemed quite familiar. Although the meeting wasn't a loving reunion, the two brothers managed to relax enough to have a decent conversation, and when they parted Rocky gave Philip a light punch on the shoulder and said, "Now keep in touch, huh?"

Philip walked Marin to Dixie and helped her in. Once he was behind the steering wheel, he turned to her and said, "So—what do you think?"

Her eyes shone with tenderness as she replied, "I think we need to have Rocky to my place one day soon for a home-cooked meal. He's too skinny."

Philip shook his head, his chest expanding with love for this beautiful, God-fearing woman. She'd seen the worst of his life, and she was ready to welcome it into her home. "Marin," he said, his voice husky from emotion, "you're willing to accept my brother?"

"You accepted mine," she pointed out. "How could I do any less for you?"

And Philip knew without a doubt she loved him. If she could look at Rocky—see the background from which he'd come—and still care for him, her love was of the daisies: loyal and pure. *Lord*, he breathed, *You've given me Your perfect gift for a wife. Thank You.*

He just needed to choose the perfect time to let her know.

eighteen

John sat on the floor in front of the Christmas tree, a fuzzy Santa hat on his head and a pile of gaily-wrapped gifts at his side. It tickled Philip to watch John open the boxes. He was so meticulous in removing the paper—first loosen the ends, then slide his finger below the edge along the bottom and finally peel the paper back away from the box. Then he would fold the paper into a neat square before looking at the contents of the box. If Philip had been an impatient man, it might have been irritating, waiting for John. But Philip didn't care if this day never ended. John could take all the time he wanted.

While John worked on one of his presents, Philip reached into his jacket pocket and removed a tiny velvet box, which he hadn't placed beneath the tree. His heart pounded, a brief concern rising as to whether Marin would accept this gift, but then he recalled every precious moment of time with her over the past months, and he knew what he was doing was right. Marin would see it, too. They'd been designed for one another.

She sat perched on the edge of the sofa, her gaze on John, a soft smile lighting her face. The twinkling red lights from the Christmas tree gave her profile a rosy glow. It took great control not to lean forward, take her face in his hands, and place a kiss on her sweetly upturned lips.

His fingers closed around the box. He held both fists outward, palms down, and nudged her lightly with his elbow. "Pick one."

She turned to look at him, her smile growing. "Does your left hand know what your right hand is doing?" she teased.

He laughed appreciatively. Bobbing both hands, he said again, "Go ahead—pick one."

With a giggle of delight she tapped the back of his right hand. He turned it over and opened his fingers, revealing the box. Her eyes grew wide, and her gaze bounced up to meet his. Her expression said clearly, *For me?*

He nodded, his heart pounding. She reached with both hands and lifted the box with her fingertips. Cradling it in her palm, she opened the lid with slow, deliberate movements, as though prolonging the pleasure. The moment the lid was fully up, she gasped and looked at him again, her eyes flooding with tears. "Oh, I'm so glad I picked that hand."

"Me, too." Philip plucked out the gold band with its single marquise diamond and slipped it onto Marin's finger, his own hands trembling. To his relief it fit perfectly. He watched as she examined it for a moment with an expression of awe; then she lifted her face to Philip. The emotion that shone from her sparkling hazel eyes took Philip's breath away. But she didn't speak to him—instead she leaned forward to gain John's attention.

John looked up, a half-unwrapped present in his lap. "Yes?"

Marin fluttered her fingers. "Look what Philip gave me."

John held Marin's hand and admired the ring. "Oooooh, it is pretty." He gave Philip a knowing look. "That must have cost a pretty penny."

Both Marin and Philip laughed.

Philip explained, "It's an engagement ring, buddy. You know what that means, don't you?"

John's face lit up. "That means you will marry Marin!"

Marin held her arm straight and admired the sparkle of the stone. Philip felt it couldn't compete with the sparkle in her eyes.

"That's right, John. I will be marrying Philip."

John gave a cheerful nod and turned his attention back to the box in his lap.

With a slight frown Marin turned to face Philip. "Philip, you do realize that I come as"—she glanced at John—"a package deal."

He shook his head, a smile tugging at his cheeks. Following his earlier impulse, he cupped her cheeks with both hands and whispered, "Ah, Marin—when will you realize I see the package as a gift?"

Marin's eyes flooded and overflowed. "Oh, Philip, I do love you."

Their kiss was salty from tears, but it took nothing from the sweetness of the moment. When they separated, Marin turned to John again. "John, when I get married, I would like very much for you to give me away."

John swung to face them, his eyes wide. "For good?" he exclaimed, obviously abashed by the thought.

Marin burst into laughter. "No, of course not. I'll always be your sister. I'll always be here for you." Briefly she explained the tradition of giving away the bride. When she finished, John nodded, a somber look on his face.

"I will do that, Marin. I will give you to Philip to be his wife." He pointed at her. "And you will be happy."

Marin leaned into Philip's embrace, and he encircled her with his arms. "Yes," she said with a contented sigh, "I will be happy."

Philip, smiling into the hazel eyes he loved, added, "God wouldn't have designed it any other way."

❧

Two months later Marin stood before a cheval mirror in a small room at the back of the church while Aunt Lenore and Aunt Chris fussed around her, straightening her veil, tightening bobby pins that held her hair in a sleek French twist, adjusting the miniature yellow rosebuds that nestled behind her left ear. Marin stood still, aware of their busyness, but somehow above it as her mind relived moments from the past weeks.

There had been times when Marin had missed her mother with an ache that was nearly unbearable, but each time she had reminded herself of how God had given her surrogate mothers—Aunt Chris, as well as Aunt Lenore and Eileen. Neither Lenore nor Eileen had her mother's meek disposition; yet their love was as evident, and Marin's heart swelled with appreciation for their steadfast presence.

Marin smoothed her hands over the sleek skirt of the trim-fitting satin gown, which her mother had worn thirty-five years earlier. Her stomach fluttered with eagerness for Philip to see her in her wedding finery. Outside the door, John waited—no doubt pacing—in his black tuxedo, crisp white shirt, and black bow tie. If her father were here, he would be the one waiting and pacing, but how proud John was of his role! She smiled, remembering the rehearsal and John's stiff, formal bearing. Although Marin missed her father, she was grateful to know he had met Philip and obviously approved of him. Dad would be pleased with her choice for a life mate.

"Well, Marin, I don't know that I've ever seen a more lovely bride." Aunt Lenore stepped back and swept her gaze from Marin's head to her toes. She turned to Chris. "Did we cover everything? Something old, something new. . .?"

Chris touched the frothy veil that lay in beguiling layers across Marin's shoulders. "The veil is new, but the dress was Mary's, remade, so we've covered the old, too."

Marin added, "And the dress covers 'borrowed' since it was originally Mother's."

"Something blue. . ." Aunt Lenore tapped her finger against her lower lip. Then she burst out, "Oh! I brought something!" She rummaged through her purse. "I must be getting old. I meant to give this to you earlier, but we've been so busy." She turned with a small, weathered jewelry box in her wrinkled hand. Tears brightened her eyes as she pushed it into Marin's hands. "Here, Marin. Your uncle gave this to me for my eighteenth birthday. You know I didn't have daughters, and this isn't something you'd give a son, so. . ." She flapped her hands, her cheeks flooding with pink. "Oh, just open it!"

Marin popped the lid to discover a sapphire and diamond pendant suspended on a dainty gold chain. "Oh, Aunt Lenore. . ." Marin raised it from the box and held it out to Aunt Chris. "Aunt Chris, look at it—it's just beautiful."

"And it isn't borrowed," Aunt Lenore inserted firmly. "It's your wedding gift from me." She paused, cupping Marin's cheeks with her hands. "You know, the sapphire is my birthstone—and your mother's. Maybe having that hang around your neck will be a remembrance of her."

Marin felt tears build. "Aunt Lenore, having you here is a remembrance of Mother—but thank you so much for this beautiful necklace. When I wear it, I'll think of both of you."

The two women exchanged an emotional hug. How Marin had come to appreciate her mother's twin!

"Here—let's put it on," Aunt Chris suggested. She fastened the tiny clasp, and then all three women looked into the mirror, admiring the bride's image conveyed there.

Marin sighed, touching the pendant where it rested in the V-neck of the lace bodice. "It's perfect. This day is perfect." Then she stomped one slipper-covered foot in impatience. "But isn't it time to go?"

As if on cue, a knock sounded on the door. Aunt Chris opened it. John stood in the doorway. He pointed at his watch, a stern look on his face. "Are you not paying attention? It is time."

Marin laughed and skipped to his side. "I'm ready, big brother. Let's go." Aunt Chris and Aunt Lenore hurried past them. The ushers would escort them to their seats as part of the wedding party. Marin slipped her hand through John's arm, and they walked together to the double doors of the sanctuary, listening for the bridge in the music that would signal her moment to enter.

Pachelbel's *Canon in D* reached their ears. *It's time!* her heart rejoiced. The ushers opened the doors, and suddenly Marin wished to prolong this moment—this sweet moment of anticipation.

But John gave her arm a little tug. "It is time," he reminded her in a raspy whisper.

She nodded, and their feet moved in one accord as they began their progress toward Marin's future.

Wedding guests rose as she and John appeared at the head of the aisle. Hurricane lanterns glowed from windowsills. White bows holding clusters of yellow roses and daisies adorned the ends of pews, the scent from the flowers mixing with those in her bouquet and creating a heady perfume that filled Marin's senses.

At the end of the aisle Philip waited, so formal-looking in his tuxedo. He'd had his hair trimmed for the occasion, giving him a dignified bearing that set Marin's heart a-pattering. How she loved this man—the man chosen for her by God. His handsome face wore an expression of joy that surely matched her own. She tried to hurry, eager to reach her groom, but John followed cues perfectly and refused to move faster than the gentle tone of the music dictated.

It seemed as though years passed before they reached Reverend Lowe, and Philip stepped near, offering his hand. But John held tight to his sister, his gaze on the minister, waiting for the precise moment to place Marin's hand in Philip's.

Reverend Lowe asked, "Who gives this woman?"

John straightened his shoulders, cleared his throat, and answered with all due solemnity. "I do." Then he pointed at Philip and added, "But not for good."

A light titter of laughter sounded from the gathered guests, but Marin knew it wasn't malicious. Marin kissed John's cheek, whispering her promise, "For ever and always, John, I'm here for you." Her heart swelled with appreciation for the man who would allow her to be there for her brother.

John kissed her back, making his own promise. "I am here for you, Marin. I love you."

John pressed her forward, into Philip's waiting embrace, then crossed to sit between Aunt Lenore and Aunt Chris. She raised her smiling gaze to Philip—her groom, her God-chosen love—and his brown eyes crinkled into an answering smile. His hand pressed warmly against the base of her spine as they turned to face the minister.

The service flowed smoothly, perfectly, and finally came the moment Marin had longed for. She and Philip faced the congregation as the minister announced, "What God has brought together, let no man put asunder."

From his spot on the front pew John asked, "What is asunder?"

Aunt Lenore sighed, fondness underscoring her tone. "Dear John. . ."

And Marin lifted her face to receive Philip's kiss.

A Letter To Our Readers

Dear Reader:

In order that we might better contribute to your reading enjoyment, we would appreciate your taking a few minutes to respond to the following questions. We welcome your comments and read each form and letter we receive. When completed, please return to the following:

Fiction Editor
Heartsong Presents
PO Box 719
Uhrichsville, Ohio 44683

1. Did you enjoy reading *Dear John* by Kim Vogel Sawyer?
   ❑ Very much! I would like to see more books by this author!
   ❑ Moderately. I would have enjoyed it more if

   _____

   _____

   _____

2. Are you a member of **Heartsong Presents**? ❑ Yes ❑ No
   If no, where did you purchase this book? _____

   _____

3. How would you rate, on a scale from 1 (poor) to 5 (superior), the cover design? _____

4. On a scale from 1 (poor) to 10 (superior), please rate the following elements.

   _____ Heroine   _____ Plot
   _____ Hero   _____ Inspirational theme
   _____ Setting   _____ Secondary characters

5. These characters were special because? _____

_____

_____

6. How has this book inspired your life? _____

_____

_____

7. What settings would you like to see covered in future
   Heartsong Presents books? _____

_____

_____

8. What are some inspirational themes you would like to see
   treated in future books? _____

_____

_____

9. Would you be interested in reading other **Heartsong
   Presents** titles? ❏ Yes ❏ No

10. Please check your age range:
    ❏ Under 18   ❏ 18-24
    ❏ 25-34   ❏ 35-45
    ❏ 46-55   ❏ Over 55

Name _____

Occupation _____

Address _____

City, State, Zip_____

Heart♥ng

HEARTSONG PRESENTS TITLES AVAILABLE NOW:

Presents

HEARTSONG
PRESENTS

If you love Christian romance...

You'll love Heartsong Presents' inspiring and faith-filled romances by today's very best Christian authors...DiAnn Mills, Wanda E. Brunstetter, and Yvonne Lehman, to mention a few!

$10.⁹⁹

When you join Heartsong Presents, you'll enjoy four brand-new, mass market, 176-page books—two contemporary and two historical—that will build you up in your faith when you discover God's role in every relationship you read about!

Imagine...four new romances every four weeks—with men and women like you who long to meet the one God has chosen as the love of their lives...all for the low price of $10.99 postpaid.

To join, simply visit www.heartsong presents.com or complete the coupon below and mail it to the address provided.

Mass Market 176 Pages

✂ —

YES! Sign me up for Heartsong!

**NEW MEMBERSHIPS WILL BE SHIPPED IMMEDIATELY!
Send no money now.** We'll bill you only $10.99 postpaid with your first shipment of four books. Or for faster action, call 1-740-922-7280.

NAME_____

ADDRESS_____

CITY_____ STATE _____ ZIP _____

**MAIL TO: HEARTSONG PRESENTS, P.O. Box 721, Uhrichsville, Ohio 44683
or sign up at WWW.HEARTSONGPRESENTS.COM**